MARY CRAWFORD

THE
Power
OF *Will*

HIDDEN BEAUTY BOOK 12

Copyright

Published on February 25, 2019, by Diversity Ink Press and Mary Crawford. Author may be reached at MaryCrawfordAuthor.com.

ISBN: 978-1-945637-51-3

Cover by Covers Unbound

HIDDEN BEAUTY SERIES

Until the Stars Fall from the Sky

So the Heart Can Dance

Joy and Tiers

Love Naturally

Love Seasoned

Love Claimed

If You Knew Me (and other silent musings)
(novella)

Jude's Song

The Price of Freedom (novella)

Paths Not Taken

Dreams Change (novella)

Heart Wish (100% charity release)

Tempting Fate

The Letter

The Power of Will

HIDDEN HEARTS SERIES

Identity of the Heart

Sheltered Hearts

Hearts of Jade

Port in the Storm (novella)

Love is More Than Skin Deep

Tough

Rectify

Pieces (a crossover novel)

Hearts Set Free

Freedom (a crossover novel)

The Long Road to Love (novella)

Love and Injustice (Protection Unit)

Out of Thin Air (Protection Unit)

Soul Scars (Protection Unit)

OTHER WORKS:

The Power of Dictation

Use Your Voice

An Everyday Guide to Scrivener 3 for Mac

Vision of the Heart

DEDICATION

To those who cope with
invisible disabilities:

You have my never-ending admiration and support.

Your battle is complicated by far too much
discrimination and doubt.

I am sorry.

Chapter One

Will

"I STILL DON'T THINK it was fair. The auctioneer shouldn't have let that lady outbid you. I mean, couldn't he tell how much you wanted it?"

"Brynley, everybody here probably wanted that car. It was a Shelby. Those are hard to come by — especially in the kind of condition that one was in."

"Aren't you mad? After all, you're William Benjamin Kordes. They should respect that," the perky college student insists as she defends my honor. Normally, I'd be all over her adulation, but tonight it grates on my nerves.

I'm not sure what's wrong with me. Brynley is smart and passionate about her work with my sister at Locate My Heart. I know her heart is in the right place and her priorities are spot on. She's beautiful and fun to hang out with. But this is our fourth date. It'll be a little more awkward to say good night tonight without making some sort of decision about where things are going.

It's not even Brynley's fault. She's been fun and

engaging, flexible and supportive — everything I should want in a partner. But the sparks aren't there. Maybe I'm just too strange and they'll never be there for me. It wouldn't be the first time my reaction to normal things in the world was completely topsy-turvy.

"What's wrong? Are you completely bummed because you didn't get the Shelby?" Brynley notices my pensive expression.

I roll my shoulder nonchalantly. "Would've been nice to add to my collection, but there are other cars."

Brynley frowns. "You're not your usual funny, witty self."

I sigh and lean back in my chair. "I'm trying to figure out what to do —"

"About your cars?"

"No, that would be a piece of cake. This is harder. I'm trying to figure out what to do about us and I don't want to hurt your feelings."

Brynley stares at me with wide eyes.

I hasten to add, "Look, it's just me. I'm weird at relationships, I guess. It's nothing you did, I promise. I like you — a lot. But I don't 'like' like you — you know, like I should if you were my girlfriend. I like you like I like my beer buddies."

Brynley snickers at me. "That's a lot of likes for a guy who's trying to tell me he doesn't like me."

"So sue me. I dropped out of college. Some days, I'm not sure English is my first language, even though it's my only one."

Brynley stands up, walks over, and gives me a big old smooch on my cheek. "Relax Romeo. When I first saw you, I thought you looked like my dream guy. I couldn't believe it when Kendall told me you were her brother. I fantasized about going out with you. When we finally did, I thought we would click like some romance novel. We clicked, for sure. But it was more like a buddy movie. I still think you are the most handsome man I've ever seen and you are like a huge overgrown teddy bear. I can't believe all the stuff you're doing with your charity — you know, the one I'm not supposed to talk about. I'm so impressed with all the things you do. I can't even get my existing technology to work, and you invent new stuff. I'm sad we're not a match — but I don't think it's anyone's fault. Sometimes, it's just not meant to be."

I breathe a huge sigh of relief and quickly gulp some of my drink as I stall to collect my thoughts. I wasn't sure how this conversation would go, but I never envisioned things going this well.

"Brynley Meeker, you are a superb human being. You deserve somebody better than me."

"Why do you say that? I just told you all the things I like about you. Were you not listening?" Brynley chastises gently.

I grimace. "See, this is what makes this whole thing awkward. You're one of the few people who actually gets me. Still, we don't have any special spark. I dunno, maybe what I see between Kendall and Jameson, Tara and Aidan O'Brien, or Heather and Tyler Colton is just a figment of my imagination."

"It's not! At first, when Kendall and Jameson got together, I was worried it was all for show. But it's totally real. Look at Phoenix and Zoe — Phoenix is cool, but even you have to admit, he's a little strange. Those two are amazing together. I think there is such a thing as a special spark with someone. Of course, I've never found it — but it doesn't mean it doesn't exist."

"I have to say, you are one of the coolest people I've ever met," I say as I grab my drink and toast Brynley. "Here's to our friendship and finding that special spark with someone — even if it isn't between us."

———————•●•———————

I slide onto my favorite stool at Joy and Tiers and order an apple fritter with some coffee. The bakery owner's honorary niece, Maddie, is chattering a mile a minute about something. She's actually pacing back and forth in her tiny bright purple wheelchair.

"But, Aunt Heather! Lexi has to have surgery in less than a month. Her grandma wants to visit, but she lives far away."

"I understand, sweetie. You can have a bake sale here anytime you'd like."

"But that's not enough! I have to think of something else too."

"What about a carwash?" I suggest. "My sister used to do a bunch of those with the band when she was in school."

Maddie looks up at Heather. "Can we please? You have a big parking lot. Grummy and Papa can bring balloons from the flower shop."

Heather looks dubious. "I don't know. Our parking lot is kind of out of the way. I'm not sure a few balloons would make too much difference. Usually, when people have carwashes, there's a whole team of people to direct traffic."

I grin as an idea occurs to me. "How would you like some help to attract attention to your carwash?"

Maddie pauses and looks up at me with wide eyes. "Are you famous like my dad?"

"No, Madeleine O'Brien, very few people are famous like your daddy."

Maddie stops spinning her chair and levels a somber stare at me. "How can you help me then?"

Awkwardly, I hop off the stool and squat beside her. "So, I understand you're raising money for something super important, right?"

Maddie nods. "Uh-huh, my friend Lexi is really sick, and she has to have surgery. She misses her grandma. I wanna surprise her and raise money so her grandma can come visit."

"I see. That's a good plan. Well, let me tell you something about myself. My name is William Kordes. I like to help people and I love to collect shiny cars. I think it would be a great idea for me to put my shiny cars on display in front of your carwash. People will stop to see my very cool vintage cars and maybe buy things at the bake sale and get their car washed at the same time."

Maddie glances up at Heather.

"I think that's a great idea. Will's cars are amazing. Can you come next Saturday? I'm sure Tyler, Denny, and Jeff wouldn't mind helping you move cars."

"What about my dad?" Maddie asks.

"Well, honey. Your daddy has a big concert Friday night. I'm not sure he'll want to get up early to be part of the caravan."

Maddie rolls her eyes. "Aunt Heather, if it has shiny cars, my daddy will like it. He's kinda like Tristan."

I choke back a laugh. "Boy, it didn't take her long to figure out the adults in her life, did it? No worries. I'll figure out a way to get them all here. Maybe I'll get Kendall to organize it. My sister is good at that kind of stuff."

I give Maddie a fist bump. "Let Operation Surprise Lexi commence!"

Bewildered, Maddie stares up at me. "That doesn't sound good."

Heather hands Maddie a cookie as she's filling up the displays. "It's okay, it's actually a good thing. Commence is just another word for start."

"Oh, let's commence then," Maddie answers with a giggle. She sets her cookie on the table and reaches up to give me a hug. "Thank you for helping me with my carwash, Mr. Will. Lexi will be so happy."

"You're welcome, Maddie. I hope we raise lots of money for your friend."

As I go back to eating my fritter and drinking my coffee, it occurs to me I've given away hundreds of thousands of dollars and received less gratitude. Sometimes, the little things count the most.

Chapter Two

Mariam

"Piper, do you think Heather would mind if I use the printer and fax machine in her office? Can you believe this employer doesn't take application materials via email? I think they forgot what decade this is. Heather is the only person I know who actually has a fax machine."

Piper laughs at my frustration. "I hear you. I feel the same way every time I have to fax an order somewhere. Some obscure places Heather orders from for the bakery don't even have websites. That's why we're still stuck in retro-land. Well, that and the fact that Heather likes to live in the middle of the last century every day by choice."

"This whole faxing thing is idiotic," I complain as I shake my hands out. My fingers are killing me from all the typing I've been doing over the last few days. "I still say a company should have minimum standards of technology compliance, you know what I mean?"

For a few minutes, the noise from Piper's industrial-strength mixer drowns out all chance of conversation. When she finishes, she turns and asks, "If this company annoys you so much right off the bat, why are you applying to work there?"

I choke on my coffee. "That's a good question. I don't know. Maybe I want a new job. Maybe I'm just tired of telling kids barely out of elementary school how to be nice to customers. I went to college so I wouldn't have to work in retail — yet here I am working at an 'upscale' department store. It's like a nightmare."

"I thought Mindy told me you came home to take care of your father after his big accident."

Leaning back against my chair, I sigh. "Initially, I did. Well, after I moved all the way across the United States for a job which never materialized. That really sucked. In many ways, my dad's accident gave me a little breathing space to recover from my shock. It's time for me to stop licking my wounds and get out there in the workforce. Otherwise, I'll be a has-been in my field before I actually get my first job."

Piper frosts a cupcake and hands it to me. "I'm so sorry. That has to be incredibly frustrating. I hope this lemonade cupcake makes you feel better."

I look at it longingly before I pop a bite in my mouth. I know I'll pay for my impulsive decision later. But my stress levels are off the chart right now. Maybe a little sugar will help my mood and release a few endorphins or something. As I take the last bite, I mentally review my application. I want to hit myself in the forehead as a thought occurs to me. "Crap! I have to run home. I forgot my transcripts. They're sitting on my kitchen table. Do you mind if I put my computer and stuff behind the counter so I don't have to carry it around? I swear I'll be right back. This stuff has to be time-stamped —"

Piper pulls off her gloves and walks around the table. She collects my computer and my accordion file and walks toward Heather's office. "I'm not worried. It'll be here whenever you need it. Go get what you need. Heather's fax machine isn't going anywhere."

Although Piper is sweet and polite, there is an undertone of censure. I blush. "You're right. I'm totally scattered right now. I swear the stress is making me stupid and rude. I'm sorry if I'm bothering you."

"Mariam, I didn't mean that at all. You seem to be putting a lot of pressure on yourself for a job you may not even want. I want you to take a deep breath and get some perspective. There's no reason to go from a job you can't stand to another job you hate."

"That's easy for you to say! You work in one of the best places in Oregon for one of the nicest people I know."

Piper shrugs. "That's true. I don't disagree. Even so, I don't have the only dream job on the planet. Sometimes, you need to wait for the right opportunity to fall in your lap."

"You sound like my sister-in-law, Mindy. She spouts stuff like that all the time. I think fate has a very unusual sense of humor when it comes to me."

—————•—————

As I walk out to my car, my body is screaming in pain. This week has been too much for me. I know I've been pushing too hard and ignoring the pitiful red flags my body has been throwing up for days ... no ... weeks on end.

My phone beeps and I growl in frustration when I

check the message. Great! Now I need to carve out time in my schedule to hire another assistant manager. This is the third one in six months. I'm starting to take it personally.

Before I reach my car, I run smack dab into a shiny red car.

"Darling, you might want to watch where you're going. Repairs for this thing cost a pretty penny."

I glance up from my phone, surprised to have encountered an obstacle and even more stunned to be dressed down by a guy who looks like he belongs on the runway at some Paris fashion show.

I swing my head around and look behind me, immediately regretting the motion as excruciating pain flies down my spine like fire. I sway from the sheer intensity. When I catch my breath, I squint at him. "Excuse me? Are you talking to me?"

"Yeah, Gorgeous. Don't see anybody else here," he quips as he slowly eyes me from the feet up, pausing to take a closer look at my chest.

I cross my arms and give him my iciest glare. "You mind?"

He raises an eyebrow. "If you don't want people to read your T-shirt, perhaps you shouldn't wear one with a saying."

Blushing, I uncross my arms. I'd completely forgotten about my T-shirt which boldly proclaims, **Waiting for awesome? Here I am**! I put it on this morning as a positive affirmation as I was filling out my application materials.

Application materials!

I nearly forgot my deadline. I got distracted by the guy's good looks and lost my focus. When I hit the button on my car, I realize Mr. GQ has me completely blocked in. Annoyed, I turn to him and growl, "Why are you parked there? In case you haven't noticed, that's not a spot."

He shrugs. "Suits my purposes."

"What purposes? You're in the middle of the parking lot!"

"Well … I'm trying to attract the attention of all the beautiful people. Seems to me it's working." He grins. My hand flies to my unruly hair which I've attempted to hide under a baseball cap. "I think you're full of it. Whatever your reason for parking your car in the middle of Heather's parking lot, I need you to move it."

The guy grimaces and runs his hand through his hair. "Sorry, I can't do that. Maddie's counting on me."

"What does Maddie have to do with this?" I snap as I angrily gesture toward his garish car.

"That sweet little girl is counting on me to be the show stopper in a grand display of my vintage cars to bring attention to her car wash."

"Oh, I just bet you love the attention. Guys like you always do."

"Huh, I wonder what it is you know about guys like me? I don't recall ever meeting you before."

I stamp my foot in frustration. "Oh … I don't know! Maybe I can guess you've never worked a day in your life and don't know what it's like to miss out on the job opportunity of a lifetime because you can't get your application materials in on time because some jerk won't move his car worth more than you'll ever make — even if you live to be a hundred and ten."

He twirls his keys between his fingers for a moment before he slides down into his low-slung car and starts the engine. He leans out the window. "You know, you should've said something."

Whirling back toward my car, I insist, "I did!"

"Funny, all I remember were a bunch of insults about my character, or lack thereof."

My head spins from utter exhaustion as I lean against my car and watch him.

The guy backs his car up about ten feet. "Sorry I bothered you. Good luck with your job search. By the way, my name is Will. For the record, I have worked several days — years' worth, in fact, during my lifetime in some of the most god-awful jobs you can imagine. Sometimes, appearances can be deceiving."

CHAPTER THREE

WILL

KENDALL SNAPS HER FINGERS in front of my face. "Will! What are you doing? You've been staring at the crossword puzzle you solved two days ago for twenty minutes. Why aren't you dressed? Aren't you going?"

I rub my hand over my chin. In all honesty, I can't remember the last time I shaved. Was it three days ago or four?

"Am I going where?" I rub my eyes with the heels of my hands.

"Phoenix and Zoe are getting married today. Did you forget?"

I glance down at my sweatpants, which are torn at the knee, and my *SpongeBob SquarePants* T-shirt. "I suppose it's blindingly obvious I forgot it was today. Zoe and Phoenix are chill, but I don't think they're quite *this* chill."

My sister sighs. "You're so lucky my fiancé is a former military man. He believes in being early. To him being on time means being late. If he wants to be early, he means obscenely early." Kendall fluffs her hair and puts on lip gloss. "I'll do my best to distract Jameson. Go take a shower. You left a suit here the last time we did a charity benefit for Locate My Heart. It's in the spare bedroom at the end of the hall. I can't do anything about the shoes, but I think you wear the same size as Jameson."

"Were you always this bossy? "

"Shut up!" Kendall pulls me down the hall. "This is for your own good. For Pete's sake, hurry up though. My powers of persuasion only go so far when Jameson is on a mission."

I salute Kendall as I grab a towel from the linen closet. "10-4. Will this be like when we were kids? Do I have to show you I washed behind my ears too?" I joke.

My sister looks at me pointedly. "No, but the long drive will give you a chance to tell me what's been eating at you for the last few days."

"I didn't tell you anything was wrong," I protest automatically.

"You didn't have to. I'm your twin sister, remember?"

━━━━●━━━━

"I cannot believe in all the craziness of getting ready, you took the time to rent a limo to get to the wedding. I'm not even sure Phoenix and Zoe have a limo. Way to upstage the bride and groom," Kendall says with an exasperated laugh.

I shrug. "Took care of that a few weeks ago. The drive to Justice Gardner's place is long and involved. I knew you wouldn't let me take one of my babies and leave the top down because it would mess up your hair. If I can't have fun, we might as well let someone else do the driving."

Kendall rolls her eyes. "I'm worried about you. I know you sold your patents — but your money won't last forever. Can you afford to be spending like this? What if you don't get any more great ideas?"

I know Kendall means no harm. Still, her words sting. No matter how many ways I try to explain how my brain works, there's simply no way to put it into words. Kendall just put my biggest fear right out there. She actually said it out loud. I hate that. I never say the words for fear I might jinx myself. So far, I've been exceedingly lucky, and my inventions have filled unmet needs in the technology world. The thought that my creative juices may dry up and one day the new ideas will stop coming terrifies me.

Pasting a smile on my face, I squeeze Kendall's hand. "You know me. I am an idea machine. My brain is full of them. I've got a whole team of lawyers, CPAs and investors looking after my money. I get to sit back and be the benevolent philanthropist who no one knows. It's actually pretty cool."

Kendall studies me so intently I know she can see right through my BS.

"If everything is so perfect in your world, why do you look like you did that time Tucker Carter gave you a black eye in the seventh grade?"

I pause for a moment to think about Kendall's question. I suppose not much has changed since the seventh grade. My issues are the same. Above anything else, I want to be liked. "I'm going to ask you a question and I want you to be honest with me. I don't want you to give me the answer you think I want to hear. I need the God's honest truth. What's wrong with me? Why is it so hard for people to connect with me?"

Kendall looks confused by my question. "Why do you ask?"

"I don't know. I had a very strange interaction with someone I've never met and it didn't go well, as usual. I wondered if I automatically send out a weird vibe or something. It was like she decided she instantly hated me. I'm trying to figure out why."

Kendall studies me for a moment and then grimaces. "Talk about a no-win situation for me. Promise me you won't get angry?"

I nod.

"If I know you, you were likely joking around. Whoever this was had no idea about your little personality quirk. To them, you probably seemed rude."

"I see your point … but I wasn't trying to be. I was just trying to be funny. She obviously didn't get the joke. She must've been having a bad day or something."

"Maybe you weren't as funny as you thought you were."

"The ironic thing is I was there doing a nice thing for Madeleine O'Brien and this woman seemed all ticked off about it. She appeared angry because I was driving the red Corvette."

Kendall rolls her eyes. "Let me guess … you were wearing your blue chambray shirt with the sleeves rolled up just so and your Ray-Bans, right?"

I nod and shrug.

My sister giggles. "Do you realize you were wearing the uniform of practically all the sleaze balls who approach us in every bar and club trying to pick us up? All you needed to complete the trifecta was a leather jacket and a few bad pickup lines."

I look out the window and watch the beautiful scenery go by for a few moments. "I might've had those too."

"For goodness sakes, Will! Do you blame the woman? She was probably in a hurry to get somewhere and you planted your gorgeousness in her way and got your feelings hurt when she didn't give you the proper respect."

My jaw drops as I regard my sister. "No way! There's no way you could have known. Heather must have told on me. That's exactly what happened! It's too bad. I didn't even get her name. Behind all the rage, she seemed like an interesting person."

"Remember, not all rage is rage. It could be pain."

"How do you know all this about a person you've never even met?" I ask skeptically.

"Technically, you don't know any more about this mystery woman than I do, other than what she looks like."

I cringe. "I think she was looking for a job and I messed it up for her."

"Did you at least apologize or do anything to make it better?"

I avert my gaze. "Not really — the situation was just awkward."

"For as much good as you've been able to do with

all your money, I liked you better before you got rich. Try to remember the person you were back then and be that guy. I think you'll have better luck."

I fidget with my cufflinks and straighten my tie. "I don't know, Sis. People thought I was strange back then too."

"But I liked that guy. I might not have understood you, but I liked you."

"You know, you're right. I miss the person I was when I had to hustle to mow lawns to keep our power on. I swore having money wouldn't change me — but maybe it has."

Kendall leans over and kisses me on the cheek. "Don't worry — deep down you're still one of the good guys. You've just forgotten what it means to be a regular guy."

━━━━◆◆━━━━

Jameson and Kendall have told me many stories about the weddings Justice Gardner has performed. I assumed most of them were highly embellished for effect. After all, Aidan O'Brien and his friends are entertainers at heart — there's bound to be a little exaggeration.

It's impossible to keep a straight face as I watch Phoenix's dog, Bruiser, remove a Kleenex from the box sitting on Justice Gardner's deck and hand it to the quietly weeping bride. Zoe turns to her soon-to-be husband in surprise. "When did you teach him that?"

Phoenix blushes. "The last time we went out to visit Mitch, we worked with his advanced class of service dogs. Bruiser must've picked up some new tricks."

Justice Gardner clears his throat. "Every time I

perform a ceremony for this group, I think I've seen everything. Somehow you all always manage to surprise me though. At my age, that's quite a feat. The two of you have decided to forgo traditional vows in favor of your own. After I got to know the two of you better, your decision didn't surprise me at all. So, I'll turn the ceremony over to the two of you."

I look around in surprise. This isn't like any wedding ceremony I've been to. I've never seen the officiant sit down with the crowd. I watch wide-eyed as the former Oregon Supreme Court Justice leans down and kisses his wife on the cheek and takes a seat. He takes the cell phone from his wife and snaps a picture of the bride and groom, then settles back to listen.

Zoe isn't wearing a veil. Instead, she has a crown of pink and white roses. Her dark hair is flowing loose and blowing in the coastal breeze. Tiny embroidered flowers trail up the skirt and bodice of her dress. She reaches out to take Phoenix's hand as they walk up to the microphone.

Phoenix is trying to look stoic, but I can tell he's having a difficult time. Abruptly he squats down and buries his hands in Bruiser's fur. Bruiser rests his head in Phoenix's lap. Collectively, the whole audience takes deep breaths with Phoenix as he calms his nerves. Being around people is not one of Phoenix's favorite things to do. He likes speaking in front of people even less. Zoe offered on several occasions just to elope, but Phoenix insisted on giving her a special day.

Slowly, Phoenix stands up. Zoe hands him the microphone as she whispers something in his ear. Whatever she said, I want someone to say that to me someday. I hope the wedding photographer caught the look of adoration on Phoenix's face. Zoe will want to frame that picture.

Phoenix watches Zoe walk over to a stool and sit down. He turns to her. "When we first met, I didn't like you." The audience erupts in awkward laughter. He pivots toward us in surprise. "Oh, that's okay. I didn't like me either. In fact, I didn't like much of anybody. I didn't know how to like people."

Bruiser flops down on the deck and stretches out.

Phoenix glances down and smiles. "This guy right here — gave me the courage to reach out and trust someone else for a change."

Bruiser looks up and wags his tail.

"Zoe thought she was rescuing a stray dog from the side of the freeway. She didn't realize she was rescuing me from myself. Don't get me wrong. As you can see, I still have Asperger's and all sorts of sensory issues. But Zoe Hurlington helped me find ways to cope and learn to like myself and other people. There was a time in my life when I didn't believe that was possible. I just figured I would be alone forever."

Bruiser gets up and puts his head under Phoenix's hand. Phoenix takes a deep breath and strokes him for a moment or two as he collects his thoughts. "Being in love with Zoe has taught me I'm stronger, braver and more connected than I ever thought I'd be."

Phoenix walks over to where Zoe is standing. "I, Phoenix Wolf, love you Zoe Hurlington with every fiber of my being. I promise to love and protect you for as long as I live."

Zoe wipes away tears before she stands up and takes the mic from Phoenix. She clears her throat. "I know Bruiser is here for Phoenix, but after those beautiful vows, I might need to borrow him."

Amazingly, she squats down in her wedding dress and gives Bruiser a brief hug. She stands up and gives Phoenix a tearful grin. "When we first met, I didn't like you either."

The audience erupts in laughter.

"To be fair, I didn't like any guys at that point. My brother had recently betrayed a woman I admired and embarrassed my entire family. Yet, they supported him and abandoned me. I trusted no one — especially guys on motorcycles who seemed too good to be true."

Bruiser moves Zoe's hand towards Phoenix.

Zoe looks down at Bruiser and grins. "Yeah, buddy, I know. I changed my mind. Lucky for you, this guy loved you." Zoe gazes back at Phoenix. "Eventually so did I. You helped me be brave and face down my own fears. You became my friend when I had none, my family when I needed one, and my protector when I felt alone. You never tried to change me into someone I wasn't. You just loved me for who I was. Phoenix Wolf, I, Zoe Hurlington love you with every fiber of my being. I will love and protect you until the day I die. I am honored to become your wife."

Phoenix brushes some hair out of Zoe's face and leans down and kisses her.

Justice Gardner quietly walks up behind them and clears his throat. "Officially, I was supposed to do a little something there — before you guys got to this point."

He turns to the audience and explains, "Zoe and Phoenix work with lots of rescue dogs. It's physical work and they don't want to risk getting their rings caught up in leashes or kennels. They've elected not to exchange rings. Instead, their friend, Jade, will give them tattoos in lieu of rings the next time they visit Florida. Like I said, every time I think I can't be surprised, something new comes along. I think it's a splendid idea. So, now as a retired member of the judiciary, I pronounce you husband and wife. Zoe, you may kiss your husband again."

From offstage, I hear Mitch, Zoe's former employer call Bruiser. Reluctantly, he gets up and obeys the command. Much to my surprise, Phoenix winks at Mitch and then dips Zoe in a theatrical movie-style dip and kisses her deeply. After he finally comes up for air, he looks up at the audience and quips, "I'm sure glad I like her now."

Chapter Four

Mariam

"Wow! I can't believe you're going to cut into that. How can you do it? It must've taken you hours to make that cake," I comment as I help Heather set out plates and little cocktail napkins at the reception.

"It wouldn't make sense for me to make the cake if no one got to eat it, now would it?" she answers with a grin.

"But it's so pretty!"

"Of course it is! I don't make ugly wedding cakes for my friends," she teases. "Calm down, Mariam. I'm a professional. I do this all the time. Everyone will survive." Heather eyes the cake and straightens a couple of flowers. "Oh, shoot! I left my favorite knife in the truck. Can you watch this and make sure none of the kids stick their fingers in the cake before the photographer gets here?"

"Sure, I'll just get the rest of the plates ready."

"The photographer should be here any minute. He was just finishing up with the bridal party."

I carefully fill a side table with little plates and cocktail napkins and arrange the silverware in a decorative pattern.

I pick up my cell phone and back away from the table as I try to imagine the shots the photographer might want to frame. I take one shot and back up to find another angle. I scream in pain as I run into a hard object and wobble on my high heels. Strong hands grab my waist and steady me.

For most people, this would not be an issue. I'm not most people. This simple act, probably meant to be helpful, sends waves of shock and pain through my body. I suddenly feel nauseous and shaky. Mercifully, someone notices and slides a folding chair under me before I collapse.

When I catch my breath, I look around to try to figure out what happened. I groan when I see the overgrown fashion model from the other day crouched near me sporting a concerned expression.

"You! Are you here to ruin another day for me? One day wasn't enough?" I demand.

"Are you okay? Did they spike the punch already? It's a little early in the day to start the party — but then again this is the beach."

I stare at him in disbelief for a few moments before I point at the area where I was just setting up with Heather. "No, I'm not drunk. The only thing I've had to drink today is good old-fashioned coffee with a chaser of H2O. Although I don't know why I'm justifying any of it to you. It's none of your business. What are you doing here? Are you stalking me?"

"Stalking you? I don't even know your name," he

protests. "You ran into me, remember?"

I gingerly take a breath as I try to breathe through the stinging pain in my rib cage. "Right. You have a point. Still, you haven't explained why you're here. Do you even know Phoenix and Zoe?"

He nods. "I don't make a habit of going to weddings between people I don't know. I find them awkward enough as it is. Phoenix works with my soon-to-be brother-in-law. We've become pretty good friends. I think their service dog training charity is so cool, I support it financially."

Heather rushes back in the reception hall carrying her bright purple toolbox. "Hi, Will! I'm glad you're here. My husband disappeared with Jeff. I need someone to move the punch bowl. Have you met Mariam Fischer?"

Will rushes over and takes the heavy toolbox from Heather and sets it on an empty table next to the wedding cake. He walks back over to us and blushes like a junior high school kid before he answers, "I've run into her a couple of times, but we haven't been formally introduced."

Heather turns to me. "You should get Will involved with your fibromyalgia awareness campaign. He's been incredibly supportive of all of our causes. He gives money to Madison's equine therapy program, Locate My Heart, and the Elliott's Houses run by Tristan and Rogue."

I raise an eyebrow and look at him skeptically. "So, what do you do? Walk around all day and hand out money to all my needy friends?"

"You make it sound like it's a bad thing — but,

yeah, that's pretty much what I do."

"Don't you have to get up and go to work like the rest of us?" I snap, feeling more than a tad envious.

"Technically, I don't ever have to work another day in my — "

"William Benjamin Kordes!" Heather exclaims. "On behalf of sisters everywhere, take my advice and put a sock in it."

Will abruptly stops speaking mid-sentence as his eyes grow comically wide.

Heather just shakes her head in dismay. "Sweetheart, you are digging yourself a swimming-pool-sized hole here. Let me try to help you before Mariam here hates you with a purple passion."

"It may be too late," I mutter.

Heather pleads with me. "Seriously, Mariam, let me try to help you. You guys weren't around when Tyler and I first got together, but we had the same kind of misunderstandings about each other. I would hate for you to get the wrong impression of William because he doesn't explain himself very well."

Heather looks up at Will. "I love you to pieces, but seriously — you need to talk to Madison or somebody about your elevator pitch or you may find yourself voted off the island."

I smirk as I chime in, "Yeah, what she said."

"So, here are a few things Will left out about himself — the reason he doesn't have to work anymore is because he is a phenomenally bright inventor. He sold his latest invention for an ungodly amount of money. Even Tristan was impressed. Despite that little car display we held the other day — one he put on to help Maddie — William has done great things with his money and taken very little credit for all he's accomplished. He's a genuinely nice guy — one of the nicest. You know the caliber of men I hang around with. I have super high standards."

I cross my arms in front of me and give Will the side eye. "It's funny how two people can meet the same person and have an entirely different experience."

Will chokes back a laugh. "I can appreciate that for the burn you meant it to be. I probably even deserve it." He looks around the large room. "Are you here with anyone?"

I blink at his odd non sequitur. "Umm, my brother and his wife are around here somewhere. I'm sure Mindy will be singing at the reception."

Will grins. "Oh great! You and I have something in common right off the bat. I'm here with my sister and her fiancé. Don't you hate being the third wheel? I mean, they always invite you to come along because it would be rude not to … but they don't really want you to stick around, right?"

"Oh my gosh! Yes! I never know what to do with myself when they get all lovey-dovey. Like do I pretend I don't notice the kiss-fest? Do I stop the conversation right in the middle and wait for them to finish whatever they're doing? It's so awkward!"

Will pulls a chair over and sits beside me. "I have a radical idea. I know I made a horrible impression on you. I'm not exactly sure what happened, but I'd like to make it up to you. Let's pretend we came to this wedding together."

My jaw drops open in shock. "Why would I do that? I'm not even sure I like you. You know you single-handedly ruined my chance to escape working at my dead-end retail job, right?"

Will leans back and loosens his tie. He sighs. "Geez! I'm sorry. I didn't mean to do anything like that. Please hang out with me today. Let me show you I'm a decent guy."

I look around the room. The photographer is busy taking pictures of the cake. Everywhere I look people are coupled up. My brother has Mindy in a close embrace and he's resting his chin on the top of her head. They look lost in their own little world. Lord knows they don't need me intruding. On the other side of the room, my mom is holding a cup of coffee for my dad and laughing at something he said. Rocco has his arm around Mallory as they talk to Donda and Jaxson. Even Heather has found her hunky husband and they appear to be deep in an animated conversation.

Fighting with indecision, I mess with a piece of my hair which has fallen out of its elaborate updo. "What if I'm uncomfortable and I want to leave?"

He hands me a card. "This is the limo driver out front. He's at your disposal."

With trepidation, I take the card from him. "This is a terrible idea. If you take limos to weddings you're not even in — you and I travel in completely different circles. In my world, the only people who have limos are the bride and groom if they're really, really lucky."

"Don't worry. I made sure Phoenix and Zoe had one too."

I roll my eyes. "I thought Heather said you were

very smart, Captain Oblivious. I'm trying to tell you about the world I occupy. In my world, we don't take limousines to our friends' weddings. In my world, I'm lucky if I have enough gas to get to work. Some days, I walk to work if gas prices are too high. That's why I was trying so hard to get a better job. Paying back my student loans is killing me." I hand the card back to him. "Good luck trying to find someone to be your plus one. I'm sure with your good looks and hefty bank account, it won't be too hard. I just don't think we would have much in common. I don't want to pretend to know things about the kind of life you lead, or to be somebody I'm not. I've had a tough month and I'm not up to a game of elaborate charades. Thanks for offering though."

"So … that's it? You're giving me the brushoff because I wanted to give my sister and future brother-in-law a treat? The roads to the coast are steep and full of curves. I wanted Kendall and Jameson to be able to enjoy themselves tonight and not worry about how they'll get home. I've got money now. I earned it. I didn't rob a bank or sell drugs to get it. I refuse to apologize for doing something nice for my family."

"I'm not asking you to. I'm merely pointing out that a guy like you would find my life boring and exceedingly tedious. I'm merely saving you the trouble of having to give me a polite brushoff later. This way, you can save yourself the time and effort. You don't even have to bother with me. You can move on to someone who is more suited to your social stature."

Will throws his head back and laughs. "That's funny. You're assuming I have social stature. Sure, more people know who I am since I sold my technology to the highest bidder, but I gotta tell you — it's not what it's cracked up to be. I thought for once in my life people would respect my skills and my ability to think through a problem and come up with a solution."

I raise an eyebrow. "I take it that's not what happened?"

Will shrugs. "To the extent anyone notices what I've done, they try to pass it off as a lucky break or get-rich-quick scheme. They don't understand I have been inventing things for as long as I can remember. I was an inventor before I had the language skills to tell people what I was up to. I know to the outside world my breakthrough invention seems like some fluke. It wasn't just a lucky accident. It was years of hard work. But nobody ever talks about that — they talk like I'm some phenom who dropped in from nowhere and got the luckiest break on the planet."

"I'm sorry they treat you that way. My brother had a similar experience. His first book was a runaway hit. He's been trying to reach the same success since then. In essence, he was lucky, and the stars aligned and all that jazz. Elijah's talent hasn't changed or gone away. The market conditions have simply changed. But I know it's frustrating for him to be chasing that ever-elusive success he once had."

"I get your brother's struggle. I can invent a million other things. But there's no guarantee I'll ever get the same success I did with a simple alternative to a phone charging cable."

"Think of it this way. There is no guarantee you won't come up with something better either."

Will walks over and stands in front of me. He

grasps my hand and kisses the back of it in a gallant gesture. "I think I love you. Are you sure you won't spend just one evening with me?"

Against my better judgment, I'm charmed by his story and his offbeat gesture. I shrug. "I hope I'm not making a bad situation worse. Keep in mind, I'm a bit like Cinderella. Late nights are tough on me."

"Your wish is my command. You just say the word and we'll be gone."

I watch with tears in my eyes as my brother accompanies his wife on the guitar. Will hands me a cocktail napkin. Gratefully, I take it from him and wipe away my tears. "Isn't it amazing? Mindy taught Elijah to play. The music seems to help calm his tics."

Will nods. "Elijah gives a guy like me endless hope."

I narrow my gaze skeptically and wait for him to continue.

"Man, you're a tough audience," Will replies with a dry chuckle. "I meant nothing derogatory, I swear. It's just that your brother is a complicated guy. It would be easy to be distracted by his Tourette's syndrome and overlook who he really is. Mindy is the perfect person to look beyond all the distractions of Elijah's disabilities and focus on who he is on the inside. That's all I'm saying. I hope one day I find someone who can look past all my limitations and idiosyncrasies and figure out who I am at the core of me too. So far, I haven't found anyone willing to look deeper than the surface and the size of my bank account. It's been disheartening at best and heartbreaking at worst."

I pick up a cracker from my plate and balance a piece of cheese on the top and gingerly eat it as I try to make sense of my tumbling thoughts. After a couple of awkward beats of silence, I decide to throw caution to the wind and plunge ahead. I deliberately step closer to Will. "If a woman was smart enough to stick around and find out who you really are behind all the masks you show the world, who would she find?"

The chaotic atmosphere in the reception hall falls away as I concentrate on Will's reaction to my question. I watch in fascination as he swallows hard and blows out a deep breath. "This will sound a little insane after all I've just said — but I'm not sure I know the answer to your question. I've spent a lifetime putting masks on. I'm such an expert at it, I'm not even sure who someone would find at the core of me."

"Seems to me if you want people to respect you for who you are, you might want to figure out who that person is," I answer quietly as I stroke my fingers across his shoulder blades.

Will looks as if I just kicked his favorite puppy. "As hard as it is to hear, I know you're right. In the meantime, do you mind if we dance?"

I smile up at him. "Isn't that the primary advantage of not being the plus one of my brother and his wife? Of course, I'll dance with you. Please be gentle. It's been many years since I've danced with anyone."

Will bows deeply. "In that case, let me show you how it's done."

"Arrogant much?" I raise an eyebrow.

Will shakes his head. "Nope. Merely confident. That song Aidan's playing? I was in his music video. His choreographer taught me enough stuff to overcome my natural tendency to have two left feet."

Grinning widely, I put my elbow out. "William Kordes, I believe we've reached the portion of the evening where you need to put up or shut up."

"Oh, I'll gladly put up. I haven't had a chance to show off for anyone in a long time. I hope you can keep up," he finishes with a wink.

CHAPTER FIVE

WILL

AS MARIAM AND I arrange ourselves on the dance floor to dance to the quirky line dance, her words echo in my consciousness. She's right. How can I expect anyone to understand who I am if I don't understand myself? I'm so lost in my thoughts, I miss the opening beat of the music and I'm immediately off step.

Mariam is trying not to let her disappointment show, but I can tell she expected better from me — after all, I set the bar sky high with all my bragging. As I struggle to find my rhythm and follow the other dancers, I'm beginning to wish I'd kept my mouth shut. Finally, Mariam takes my hand and deliberately shows me the next step. I blush to the roots of my hair as I fall into step beside her.

So much for showing off.

I take a deep breath and let it out as I try to relax into the fun country tune and enjoy myself. As I let the music wash over me and allow my muscle memory to take over, I grin with joy.

Mariam notices my newfound enthusiasm and winks as she adds a flourish to her step. For a couple of minutes, our dance moves are completely synchronized. It looks as if we've been dancing together for months — you would never guess we only officially met tonight. Mariam lets out a peal of laughter when we successfully complete a particularly challenging sequence of steps. "Okay, I may have to eat my words, GQ, you're pretty good at this." I pull her closer for a spin and place my hand in the small of her back. Geez, she smells amazing!

Her nickname almost makes me miss a step. "GQ?" I ask.

Mariam flushes. "I can't believe I said that out loud. It's what I call you in my head. You always look like you should be strutting down a runway somewhere."

I stroke my chin self-consciously. "I have little to do with my looks. It's an accident of my gene pool. Have you looked in the mirror recently? You look amazing!"

This time, Mariam stumbles. "Umm, thanks. I feel awkward because I've been growing my hair out forever. It's always sticking out somewhere."

"Trust me, you look gorgeous."

I'm so focused on my conversation with Mariam, I fail to see the couple in front of us lose their footing during a spin until it's far too late. Out of the corner of my eye, I see the large man in a western shirt careen toward Mariam with frightening speed. I reach out and grab her arm to steer her out of the way. She shrieks in pain and falls to the floor. I curse under my breath. He must have struck her. My timing always did suck.

When I squat by her side to help her, she is

crumpled in a ball. Her beautiful dress is wrapped awkwardly around her legs. Mariam is clutching her arm and tears are rolling down her face. Instinctively, I pull her dress down so it covers her legs and reach out to help her sit up. "Are you okay? Let's get ice on that."

"Please, don't touch me," Mariam pleads as the music comes to an abrupt halt.

I step back, uncertain about how to help. "Oh man, I'm so sorry. I should've been quicker on my feet."

Elijah and Mindy push their way through the crowd on the dance floor.

"Jigger, jig, jig, what happened here, Sis?" Elijah asks as he surveys the scene.

Mariam winces. "Our line dance turned into a mosh pit. I was in the wrong place at the wrong time."

Elijah reaches out and offers his hands to Mariam. His move isn't so different from what I tried to do, but she accepts her brother's help. I notice he's counting as he serves as a counterbalance. "Jigger, jig, jig, ready? One, two, three … up you go."

When Mariam sways on her heels and Elijah places a hand on her shoulder to steady her, Mariam gasps in pain.

"I apologize. I guess I should've made sure there was more space between the rows when we were dancing," I ramble. I look around to see if I can find the guy who caused the injuries. The way Mariam is holding her arm, I wonder if he fell onto her with more force than I realize. Maybe he busted it or something.

Mindy looks startled by my statement. "Will, some things aren't your fault, even if it seems like they are." She turns to Mariam. "Do you want us to grab you some cake and something to drink so you can take your anti-inflammatories?"

Collapsing into a chair, Mariam leans her head back against the wall and uses a cocktail napkin to wipe away tears from the corners of her eyes. "I hate to be a party pooper, but I just want to go home. Honestly, I am out of spoons."

Mindy nods sympathetically. "I understand. Let me tell Aidan I won't be singing with the band. I'll be right back."

"Gah! I hate this. You guys don't have to leave on account of me. You should stay here and enjoy the party. You guys never get the chance to be anonymous anymore. You should totally take advantage of that. I'll just catch a ride with Uber or something and get the driver's recommendation for a place to stay."

Tentatively, I step closer and squat down next to Mariam. "I was being honest when I told you the limousine is at your disposal. If you need to take it to get home, that's fine."

She regards me as if I'm some reptile slithering across the floor. "I think that would probably be best. I knew a guy like you would never understand."

Elijah takes another chair and scoots it across the floor. He turns it around and straddles it backward. He stares intently at his sister until she reluctantly meets his gaze. "Jigger, jig, jig, now Mari, I know you and I jigger, jig, jig don't always see eye to eye, but what you're asking isn't fair. You can't expect the guy to understand what he doesn't know. That would be like me expecting Mindy to know all about Tourette's without telling her anything about it."

Mariam's eyes are bright with anger. "It's different with you. People can always tell something is wrong with you. It's obvious from the second you open your mouth. Nobody believes anything is wrong with me. The doctors can't even agree. Many of them think I'm crazy! Why should I tell this guy? He'll probably think I'm crazy too."

A flush comes over Mindy's face as she straightens her spine. "I'm trying to be nice because I know you hurt. With all due respect, shut your mouth about my husband. Just because you're his sister doesn't mean you have the right to be cruel."

"I'm sorry. This is all my fault. I should've never ventured out on the dance floor. I'm not actually that good. I should have guessed someone would get hurt. I didn't mean to start a family argument," I interject.

Mindy whirls around on me. "No! This is not your fault and if my sister-in-law is honest with herself, she knows that too. You both are stronger than you think you are."

Mariam rolls her eyes. "Yeah, right! Not feeling so strong right now." She points to a dusky area on her forearm which looks suspiciously like my hand print.

The blood drains out of my face as memories of my mother's bruised body play like some sick slideshow. "I'm going to leave now. I've hurt you twice in less than twenty minutes. You're right. You're safer without me," I stammer as I turn to leave.

"Mariam, don't do this to him, jigger, jig, jig. Will is a great guy. He does phenomenal things for our community. Jigger, jig, jig, he deserves to know the truth."

I swallow hard. "Elijah, I appreciate your vote of confidence, but in my experience when people find out the truth of who I am, they rarely stick around anyway. Your sister's first instincts are probably correct. Tell Phoenix and Zoe I'm sorry for creating a scene at their wedding. For the record, I had a great time tonight, Mariam. Thanks for letting me just be me for a while."

━━━━●━━━━

Adrenaline surges through my body as I run down the beach. Fortunately, it's late at night, and there aren't very many tourists out. The few that are don't seem to think it's odd that I'm running in a suit. I chuckle softly. That's Oregon for you. Anything goes here.

After I exhaust myself, I run up to one of the sightseeing paths and sit on a concrete bench and reflect on tonight's events.

Truth. What a funny concept. It means completely different things to everyone.

Until tonight, I would've sworn on every car I own that I am nothing like my no-good father, Norman Kordes. I would never hurt a woman. Yet, tonight I did, and she has the marks on her body to prove it. Worse yet, the excuses coming out of my mouth sounded just like my old man. I didn't mean to … I was just clumsy … I didn't know my own strength. How many times did I hear those words come out of my father's mouth as Kendall and I were trying to patch our mother back together after one of my father's insane rampages?

Truth. My mother has a tenuous relationship with the truth. She wouldn't know what it was if it came up and bit her in the butt. She likes to pretend everything is fine, even when the world is collapsing around her. Even after all these years, she excuses the abuse my dad put her through. Either she pretends it never happened, or she blames it on his military service.

One day my dad went out for beer and never returned. It almost destroyed my mom and Kendall. My sister doesn't trust men much between what my dad did and what happened after her son died from SIDS. She might be my twin, but we couldn't be more different. Kendall misses him a great deal, but frankly, most of the time, I'm glad my dad is gone because he's not hurting my mom anymore.

Okay, truth is there's a part of me who wants to find him if only to ask the jerk what was more important than his family? I want to ask him if he knew Kendall and I were taking odd jobs in junior high and high school so our electricity wouldn't be shut off? My mom still pretends he'll come back any day now. I don't know what to believe.

When I first struck it big with my invention, I hired a private investigator. He wasn't the same caliber of anyone who works for Identity Bank and he didn't turn up anything. I remember being more disappointed than I expected to be. Back then, I chalked it up to being bummed that I couldn't show my old man I had become something despite his predictions I was nothing but a weird loser.

What started out as a search to appease my mother and my sister has suddenly taken on a sense of urgency. I need to find answers. I need to find the truth. I have to figure out once and for all what made my father turn into a monster because it seems I've inherited more than just my good looks.

The Power of Will

Sometimes, the truth hurts.

CHAPTER SIX

MARIAM

I TAKE A DEEP breath and inhale the rich scent of leather as I sink back into the luxurious seat and adjust the seatbelt.

Holy cow! I can't believe I'm actually riding in a limousine like I'm a member of the royal family or something. But even as the thought crosses my mind, a feeling of remorse sets in. I can only imagine what this experience would have been like with my witty wedding companion with his infectious laughter and compassionate spirit.

He's not here and I have only myself to blame.

Myself and my stupid fear of letting anyone close because of the F word.

Oh, no, not *that* F word, although I say it plenty under my breath.

Fibromyalgia. That F word. An F word people don't even agree exists.

I look just fine. By looking at me you'd never guess there's anything wrong with me. But when I'm having a flare, I feel eighty. My body feels like it's on fire and sometimes it feels like vises are pulling my joints apart bit by bit like I'm on some medieval torture device. That's what's happening right now. So, instead of enjoying my friends' wedding, I'm putting on a happy face and trying to pretend I'm not completely falling apart on the inside.

That's not exactly true. I didn't pretend well. Let's be honest. I was a witch to a person who didn't really deserve it.

Morosely, I look out the window and notice the beautiful sunset. "Do you mind if we take a loop closer to the beach so I can take a few pictures?" I ask the limo driver.

"Sure thing. One of the scenic overlooks just up the road a piece is one of my favorites."

I remember what it was like before my brain glitched out — when I was the life of the party. I was always the first to arrive and the last to leave. I could dance without fear of colliding with anyone. I didn't have to hide my emotions or pretend to be anything I wasn't. I could be open and honest. I miss that person. Pain, and the fear of pain, has turned me into someone I don't even like. I crave the sense of joy and freedom I once had.

The limo slows and turns off Highway 101. "Would you like me to lower the windows, miss?"

Startled, I answer the driver, "Umm, sure. It would be easier to take pictures."

"Let me pull right up here. There's a great lookout spot."

As I take panoramic pictures, a familiar figure

comes into focus. As I look closer, I recognize the classic dark suit I was cuddled up next to a couple of hours earlier while I was dancing.

Abruptly, I open the door and awkwardly make my way out of the luxury vehicle. "Do you need any help?" the driver asks.

"No, I'm good. I'll be right back," I respond as I walk toward the solitary figure sitting on the bench. My cute wedding shoes are not making this task easy. When I reach his side, he appears to be lost in thought. I cough softly. "Want some company?"

"Mariam? I thought you would be halfway home by now."

"I thought so too. The lure of the beach turned out to be irresistible and my family took forever to say goodbye at the wedding. My mom and dad wanted to make sure I was okay before they let me go."

"I don't blame them for being worried. I left a heckuva mark on you. They probably don't want me in the same state as you."

A gust of wind kicks up and my hair blows in my face. My dress whips around my ankles. I shiver. Will takes off his jacket and drapes it around my shoulders. "Let me take a couple pictures of the sunset. After I do that, I need to explain a bunch of stuff to you."

I take my phone out of my purse and take several pictures.

Will watches me for a moment or two. "Explain what? That I was a careless jerk who couldn't keep you safe at your friends' wedding? I already know that. I hurt you once and then I hurt you again. There's no excuse for that."

The look of self-hatred on his face is heartbreaking. I have to intervene. I slip my phone back into my purse and place my hand on his forearm. "Do you mind if we go back to the limousine? I'm getting a little chilled. This is going to take a while."

Will gallantly offers his arm to steady me as we walk back toward the limo. He helps me get in and then sits beside me. "I honestly thought I would never see you again."

"Not a huge surprise, considering I was beyond rude."

When I shiver, Will takes a blanket from under the seat in front of us and tucks it around my legs. "It's not like I didn't give you a reason —"

"No! That's what I need to explain. None of this is your fault."

Will shakes his head and opens his mouth to argue.

I hold up my hand to stop him. "Look, I know we were dancing and there was a collision, but it didn't cause all this damage. That's what Elijah and Mindy were hinting at when they were urging me to tell you the truth. You know — spoons and all that?"

Will fidgets with his collar before he faces me. "I'm sorry, I don't have a clue. I don't know anything about your family secrets or what you mean about spoons. Am I supposed to?"

"'Spoons' are simply a tool to talk about how much energy people with chronic illness burn while we do seemingly simple tasks. Most normal people don't even have to think about it because taking a shower or going to the doctor isn't exhausting. They have energy to spare but people like me measure it out by the spoonful. So, we often sit around and do nothing to conserve our 'spoons'. Everyday activities — even fun ones — can burn through spoons like nobody's business."

I lean my head back against the seat and wince when a bobby pin pokes my head. All the stress of the day hits me, and I begin angrily pulling at all the pins in my hair. Tears well up in the corners of my eyes as I inadvertently pull my unruly hair.

Placing his hands over mine, Will stills my frantic movements. "You mind?"

Mutely, I shake my head.

He gently runs his fingers through my hair as he removes all the clips and pins. As he does one last check, he gently massages my scalp then combs his fingers through to the end. "You have gorgeous hair. It feels like silk," he says as he sticks the hair accessories in his jacket pocket. "Does that feel better?"

"How did you get so good at that? Are you secretly a hairdresser or something?"

Will throws back his head and laughs. "Ha! Sometimes it seemed like that. When we were kids, we didn't have a lot of money. When I took my mom to the doctor, I would look at the magazines in the waiting room to try to learn all the tips to help Kendall fit in. Don't ask her about the time in the sixth grade when I took the neighbor's curling iron out of the trash and rewired it though."

"Oh?"

He shrugs. "I was new to refurbishing. I thought I was improving it and I made it a little too hot. Let's just say Kendall got a new shorter hairstyle. She didn't talk to me for weeks."

I shake my hair out, take my shoes off and tuck my feet under me as I try to relax. "Speaking of talking, this is probably as good a time as any. How much do you know about medical stuff?"

"I know some stuff. Not as much as I probably should. I had seizures as a kid and Kendall lost her son to Sudden Infant Death Syndrome a few years back. I wasn't around when it happened, but I did some research to try to figure out why my nephew died and why, of all the people on the planet, it had to happen to my sister. Well, you can probably figure out that I found out positively squat about that. There were no great answers. At first, I wanted to blame Kendall's fiancé because he was babysitting. But it wasn't really his fault either."

"I'm sorry that happened to your family. It's so hard when there are no answers. Everyone wants to blame themselves."

"These days, I tend to stick closer to technology. Computers and mathematics are predictable. Logic suits me. The mysteries of the human body frustrate me because nothing is consistent."

I can feel myself shrinking into my body as the impact of his words strike me. "I've got horrible news for you. You will absolutely despise me. Absolutely nothing about me is predictable or easy to figure out."

"What do you mean?" Will studies my change in demeanor.

"Like I said, what happened to me wasn't caused by some random collision on the dance floor." I show him the bruised, swollen area on my arm. Will recoils and blanches. "See this reaction to what should have been a simple mishap?"

He nods as he looks like he's about to pass out.

"I have no control over my body's reaction to a simple collision at my friends' wedding or anything else for that matter. My body is attacking itself at an alarming rate. I have fibromyalgia. Sometimes it's manageable and barely noticeable. Other times, like tonight, I am in a full-blown flare. Simple things like your hands at my waist to prevent me from falling, a hug from a friend, or the pressure from a hair clip on my scalp can cause me immense pain."

"Why didn't you say something? The last thing I want to do is cause you pain." Will carefully moves away from me.

"That! That right there. That's why!" I cry as I point to the distance between us. "I'm so sick of that! I want my life to be like it was before! I want a boyfriend who can hug me and kiss me with abandon. I want to be able to dance without wondering if I'll bump into my partner or gasp with pain. I need to be able to kiss someone without worrying whether it'll hurt my neck or bring tears to my eyes."

"What about your doctors? Can't they do something?"

Tears of frustration leak down my face as I scoff, "You would think so, right? This is the world where we transplant arms and faces and where women who are sixty can have babies. Yet, in my world, I can't even convince all the doctors I'm actually sick."

Will's eyes widen with surprise.

"Oh sure, there are a few who believe that fibromyalgia is a real illness and they are working really hard to come up with effective treatments. But even so, it presents so differently in each individual it's hard for them to come up with a treatment regimen. What worked last week can send me into a full-blown flare this week. I've started on protocols which seemed promising only to find that after a while the medicine that was supposed to help me made my symptoms worse."

"Why wouldn't they believe you're sick? Can't they simply look at your bruises and run a test?"

"Believe it or not, there is no definitive test for fibromyalgia. It's more like a scavenger hunt. The doctors have to eliminate everything else that it possibly could be and, if there's nothing else left, if they're open-minded, they might support a diagnosis of fibromyalgia."

"*That's crazy!* We can fight cancer on a gene level now. How can they not have a test for something as devastating as fibromyalgia?"

"I don't know, Mr. Inventor. Maybe you can tell me?"

"I wish I had the brains to be in the medical field. I just invent gadgets no one has thought of before. Is it a matter of getting you to the right experts?"

"I wouldn't know. I don't have that luxury. Crappy job with even crappier insurance, remember? I see who I see and hope for the best."

"Can't your brother help? I was under the impression he was doing pretty well—"

I pull as far away from Will as I can and cram myself in the corner of the limo as I stare at him in disbelief. "You're kidding, right? Do you have any idea what my family has been through? I would never ask my brother to help me! I am not his responsibility! I'm not a charity case!"

Will puts up his hands in protest. "I didn't mean that as an insult. I only meant Elijah seems like a standup guy. He doesn't seem like someone who'd sit comfortably on the sidelines."

I chuckle but can't keep the sarcasm out of my voice. "You don't miss much, do you? No, you're right. Elijah would be more than happy to fix everything if he could. When my dad was nearly killed by a madman at his job, Elijah dropped everything and moved home. He had the means to afford a private bodyguard and therapist. All I could do was help my mom take care of my dad. It didn't seem like much in comparison."

"So you don't want his help?" Will asks with a puzzled expression.

"It doesn't matter if I want his help or not, I'm not asking. I don't want to be a burden. That's not who I am. This stupid disease has changed our relationship enough. Asking for help is a step too far. Elijah has his own problems. He's got his own family now and he recently launched a publishing company. Being an artist is risky enough. He doesn't need to feel responsible for me."

Will shoots me a ghost of a smile. "Okay, I get it. I know Kendall doesn't share a bunch of stuff with me either because she doesn't want me to worry."

I smile. "That's nice."

"Speaking of nice, I have a reputation for being nice. I could help you."

My jaw drops open. I slap my hand over my mouth

after I blurt, "Are you learning impaired?"

Will's eyes bug wide open. "I beg your pardon?"

"Okay, okay … maybe I could have been more polite — but Geez Louise! I just told you I'm not some pathetic charity case and then you go and say something like that."

"I know you're not a charity case. Maybe I think you're cool and I like you. Maybe I don't want to see you hurt and in pain and I want to help you get better."

"Why would you want to do anything for me? I was rude to you — like more than rude. If my *Bubbe* was still alive, she would've washed my mouth out with soap just to make a point if she would've seen the way I treated you."

"*Bubbe*?" Will questions.

"Oh, it's a Jewish word for grandmother."

"Oh, gotcha. We called ours Mawma. She's been gone a while." Will shifts so he's facing me. Even in the dim light, I can tell his gaze is intense. "If you were rude to me — and I'm not saying you were — but if you were, I had it coming. After all, I made you late for your job interview. I didn't listen to what you were telling me that day. If it weren't for me, you might've gotten a better job with killer insurance benefits. I literally stood in the way of that. I guess you could say I owe you one."

I blush to the roots of my hair. "Umm … about that … I may have overstated things slightly. You didn't sabotage an actual job interview. I was using Heather's fax machine to apply for a job. They wanted a whole freaking essay about why I was qualified. I forgot my transcript at home, so I was running late."

Will runs his hand through his hair making it stick

straight up. "I hate applications like that! Can you believe I had to fill out one like that to work at a pizza joint? Why were you faxing it anyway? Why not submit it online like everyone else?"

I snicker. "Would you believe the company wouldn't accept online applications?"

"I know I'm a tech junkie, but that would've ruled them out for me. Who knows, they probably didn't even have health insurance benefits if they're that backward."

"I don't know. It was hard to do much research on them. Their web presence was minimal."

"How did you find out about this job?"

"There was an ad in the classifieds."

Will's jaw tightens. "Did you have Jameson run a background check on them?"

I hang my head for just a moment before I stiffen my spine and meet his gaze. "No! I don't need my brother's friend's permission to look for a job. Pfttt! It was a foot-in-the-door sort of job. It was just a research assistant position. I was hoping once I got there, they would see how qualified I was — and I would be offered a better job … eventually. Anything would be better than working at the mall."

"Just for fun, pretend this is the job interview I robbed you of. Mariam Fischer, tell me why you are the perfect employee for my company?"

"Oh, come on, Will! Today has been exhausting and I hurt from head to toe. Do you really need to torture me like this? I'm not great at talking about myself — even on a good day."

"I promise this won't be as bad as the idiotic essay

questions like, 'If you were a tree, what kind of tree would you be?' Pretend I'm an executive of a company you've always wanted to work for, and you and I have a really long elevator ride up to the top floor. You've got three minutes to persuade me to hire you. Miraculously, there's no one else in the elevator and I am a captive audience. Tell me what skills you'll bring to my company I won't be able to find anywhere else."

"Okay, Mr.——?"

Will shrugs. "You can just call me Ben. I work for Hallway Innovations. Give me your best pitch."

I nervously fold the fabric of my skirt between my fingers as I try to plan what I'm going to say. "It's nice to meet you, Ben. I am Mariam. I graduated with a degree in sociology and anthropology. In graduate school, I studied genetics and migration. I am very organized and I'm great at solving problems. I have a keen eye for detail and my personal circumstances have given me the ability to be compassionate and understanding to other people's stress and problems. I am a self-starter. If your business needs something done, I can figure out how to accomplish it, even if you are too busy to give me direct instructions."

"Does that mean you are difficult to work with?"

My eyes widen and I swallow hard as I try to decide how honest to be. I take a deep breath and let it out as I relax. This is only pretend, so what could I possibly have to lose? Honesty for the win. I'd never be this brave in a real job interview. But, this is fantasyland — we're sitting in the back of a limo, after all.

"Under most circumstances, you'll have no problem working with me. However, if you discriminate against other people or treat them cruelly, you will hear from me. I don't abide that kind of behavior. If your business is on the up and up, I will be your happiest camper. If you con people out of money or don't pay your employees or contractors fairly, I will be the squeakiest wheel you've ever encountered."

Will covers his mouth with his hand as he chokes back a laugh. "I see, Ms. Fischer. I admire your conviction. Is there anything else you would like to add?"

The limo driver turns on some interior lights. I take advantage of the subdued lighting as I try to read Will's expression. Much to my frustration, he is giving nothing away as he waits for my answer. I try to gather my wits around me as I compose a response.

"I guess I should tell you I'm not a quitter and I don't give up easily. I've worked for three years at a job I absolutely despise because I gave them my word I'd do my best until I found something better. So far, I haven't been able to find anything. Therefore, I'm still working at a place I detest until I get another job because I'm loyal and true to my word."

I lean back against the leather seat and wipe tears out of the corners of my eyes with the heels of my hands. "Can we stop now?" I whisper. "I've had about all I can take."

"I've heard what I need to hear. Sit back and relax."

"What was the point of that?" I demand with more than a little snark. "Was it fun to make me feel like a fool?"

"Not particularly. But this is…"

"What is?"

"Mariam Fischer, I cordially invite you to join our team at Hallway Innovations as the grant coordinator. The position comes with a generous pay package complete with premium health and life insurance benefits."

Without meaning to, I gawk behind me to make sure there's not another person behind me named Mariam waiting to accept this ludicrous offer.

"I'm not sure I understand. I told you about my fibromyalgia and how it impacts my ability to work. Some days, I have this weird brain fog. It's like thinking through fiberglass insulation. Not much thinking goes on during those days. It's part of the reason I don't have a more challenging job right now."

"Oh, I get it. I'm okay with that. You're not the only person with challenges. Hopefully, with proper medical insurance, you get some relief from your symptoms."

"But what if I don't? What if I get worse? Are you prepared to take that kind of risk? Is your boss?"

Will laughs out loud. "Mariam, were you listening when Heather introduced me?"

I clear my throat nervously. "Not really. I was still a little thrown to see you at Zoe's wedding."

"My name is William Benjamin Kordes. Hallway Innovations is my company. The name is a rather sarcastic nod to the number of times I was thrown out of class as a kid. I never fit in. So, the teachers never knew what to do with me. They used to make me move my desk out to the hallway while they taught class. I used that time to invent things — all sorts of things. My most famous invention, you know the one that made me rich, was invented during one of my extended stays in the hallway. I know what it's like to be different. I'm okay with that. If we have to work around your limitations that's what we'll have to do."

"But what if it means I can't do my job?"

"I'm no lawyer, but I believe I'm supposed to find ways to help you do your job."

"Yeah … but not everybody does that. I learned that lesson the hard way when my research position disappeared after they found out about my health condition."

"That's not gonna happen. After all, you already told me I'd never hear the end of it if I treated someone unfairly. My company has a vested interest in a good public image. I'm not messing that up. Besides, despite our rough start, I really am a nice guy. So, Ms. Fischer, can I count on you to be my newest employee?"

I twist my belt around my finger. "You have no idea how much I hate working at the mall. Still, you have to promise me that if I am not pulling my weight, you'll tell me, okay?"

"It's a deal — as long as that's a two-way street. If you need anything from me, let me know."

I wrap my arms around my middle as my head pounds.

"I hate to ask, but I need to find a place to crash. I'm not sure how much longer I'll be able to stay upright."

Will cringes. "I should've thought of that. Let me call around to get you a room at a local hotel. Relax, I'll take care of everything."

As Will pulls out his phone and begins to talk to

someone on the other end, I drift off. For the first time in a very long time, I trust that someone else will take care of things. It feels like a million pounds of weight have been taken off my shoulders. The power of Will is frightening, but it's also a bit intoxicating.

CHAPTER SEVEN

WILL

JUST AS I FINISH hooking up the last monitor in my new office space about a half-mile from Identity Bank West, Elijah knocks on the door frame. "Jigger, jig, jig, can I talk to you for a minute?"

I look up at him and grin. "Sure. I always forget how fast news travels in such a small town. What do you think?"

Elijah glances around. "Well, jigger, jig, jig, you work fast, that's for sure. So much for working behind-the-scenes — this is a mighty public statement, jigger, jig, jig."

I chuckle. "I never made a big secret of the fact that I invent things. Hallway Innovations was always part of the public record. Until now, I've kept the charitable foundation under wraps for personal reasons."

"Jigger, jig, jig, I hope you don't mind, I came to see what you had planned when it comes to my sister."

"What do you mean?" I ask as I sit on one of the rolling chairs and adjust the seat.

"Jigger, jig, jig, I've got a couple questions, that's all."

"Oh, I get it. The big brother routine — ask away."

"Jigger, jig, jig, actually I'm the little brother. But, it's the same concept jigger, jig, jig. I just don't want my sister to be taken for a ride. She's been disappointed before. I don't want her heart to get broken again."

"It's a job offer, Elijah. I'm a decent guy. I thought you knew that."

"I want to believe you, jigger, jig, jig — but this is Mariam we're talking about. She doesn't look it, but she's fragile. Jigger, jig, jig, she would kill me if she knew I said that. Is this a legitimate job offer? I hope so. Jigger, jig, jig, my sister is brilliant. Jigger, jig, jig, you know that, right?"

"I've got a clue, otherwise I wouldn't have hired her."

"So this is a real job, jigger, jig, jig? Not one you made up so you can date my sister?"

I take a long drink from my sports bottle before I meet Elijah's gaze. "Honestly, your sister is all kinds of cool and she's absolutely stunning. I would be totally into her if she was interested in me — but Mariam has made it abundantly clear she is definitely not into me. In fact, I think she probably hates my guts. For some reason, I stand for everything she despises."

Elijah lets out a snort of laughter. "Jigger, jig, jig, I see my sister held nothing back during her job interview. So, if she hates you, why did you bother to hire her?"

"You can probably relate to this. Now that I'm rich, it's hard to find people who will tell me the truth. People tend to tell me what they think I want to hear.

Your sister is not one of those people. I need someone to tell me the unvarnished truth. Sometimes my inventions completely miss the mark or my pitch for them is terrible. I'm often too close to the project to recognize that. I've got good financial people and solid advisors. However, sometimes I doubt their ability to stand up to me."

Elijah nods knowingly. "Jigger, jig, jig, I hear you. Sometimes you need honesty more than you need cheerleaders."

"I struggle even more with the charity side of my business. You should see the stories that come in. They all break my heart. I have a hard time deciding which ones to help. Intellectually, I know there are people who scam the system, but there's still a part of me which doesn't want to accept that."

Elijah grins widely. "If you need someone to be a skeptic, jigger, jig, jig. Mariam is a natural. Jigger, jig, jig, I don't want to say she's a glass half empty kind of gal, but she's been burned so many times she's learned to be extraordinarily cautious."

"That's good. Sometimes I have so much fun playing the fairy godfather I forget to have a reality check every now and then."

His expression sobers quickly. "Jigger, jig, jig, speaking of reality checks, what you saw at the wedding the other day is only a small taste of what can happen to Mariam. Her health can crash and burn quickly — without notice." Elijah grimaces. "Jigger, jig, jig, maybe I shouldn't have said anything. I don't want you to take away the only decent job offer she's had in years."

I stand up and put my hand on Elijah's shoulder.

"As far as I'm concerned this whole conversation is just between us. I won't withdraw my job offer. I knew about Mariam's fibromyalgia before I offered her the position. I'll tell you the same thing I told her. Whatever happens, we'll work around it. Hopefully, with access to better medical care, they'll be able to treat her condition and she'll feel better."

"Jigger, jig, jig, I know you mean well. First, I'd be shocked if Mariam allows you to help her. After I got my big publishing deal, I tried my best, but my big sister is fiercely independent, jigger, jig, jig. But even if she does, I'm not sure if all the help in the world can fix her. I don't want you to be disappointed if what she has isn't fixable, jigger, jig, jig."

I swallow hard. "When I was a kid, I mowed other people's lawns and took out their trash to keep the electricity on and buy my mom's medication. I swore up and down that if I ever got rich, I would make it so that everyone who needed heat in their house or needed to go to the doctor would always have the chance to. Now you're telling me even that dream wasn't big enough?"

Elijah shakes his head. "No, that's not what I'm saying at all. Your dream is phenomenal, jigger, jig, jig. It's just that people like Mariam and me — you know, the different ones — we deserve to be loved and respected just the way we are … without being fixed."

Elijah's simple words hit me like a roundhouse kick to my chest. No wonder Mariam is so angry with me.

She had good reason.

I reach out to shake Elijah's hand. "Thank you so much for stopping by. You have given me a lot to think about. I promise to do my best to treat your sister right.

If you have concerns, stop by anytime."

Elijah shakes my hand. "Don't worry. Mariam's bark is worse than her bite. You guys will do fine."

—— ●◆ ——

I've been less nervous giving presentations to the biggest tech companies in the world than I am showing Mariam the new office.

Mariam wrinkles her nose. "It smells weird in here. Did they recently lay new carpet?"

I toe the discrete forest green carpet with my tennis shoe. "I wouldn't know. I've only been here a few days."

Her brow wrinkles. "Where were you before?"

"This is going to sound much worse than it really is, but I've been operating from my sister's basement."

Mariam's eyes open so wide she looks like a cartoon character.

"Wait a minute! You told me to be careful of the other company because they might be a scam and now you tell me you work out of your sister's basement? What am I going to do? Holy Cow! I left my job! It might've been crappy, but at least I had a steady paycheck and some sort of benefits — even though they were terrible. I wonder if I burned every bridge I had there? Oh my gosh! I can't believe I did this again."

I take Mariam by the hand and lead her over to a leather couch in the waiting area. "Please sit down and let me explain."

She nods tightly. "This better be good. I'll be pissed off if I screwed up my life again by letting a handsome man with a pretty smile spin promises he can't keep."

"I know it sounds bad, but I swear to you, Hallway Innovations is more than solvent. So am I, for that matter."

"So … why the poor man routine?" Mariam asks as she perches on the edge of the couch. She looks ready to bolt at any second.

I pat the back of the couch. "You might as well make yourself comfortable, this will take a while. Do you want something to drink?"

Mariam shakes her head. "I just want to figure out what's going on. I need to know if I have to start over from scratch. My parents have been to hell and back over the past few years. I'd hate to have to go to them for help. I'm a little old for that, you know what I mean?"

"I do know. I promise I'm not some grifter taking you for a ride. I've been there and I wouldn't do it to someone else."

"You're a rich guy! How could you possibly know what it's like to wonder how you will pay the rent?"

"I'm rich now. But it wasn't always that way. I guess that's why, as you say, I live like a poor person. I've never thought of it that way. I spend my money on things I like. You probably noticed I have a thing for cars. So, I invest in collectible cars. A couple years ago, Kendall was having a tough time, and I came to Oregon to help her out. There's a lot of snow in Nebraska. I decided I liked it here better. So, I moved here."

"What about the rest of your family?"

I grimace. "That's kind of a long story. I tried to convince my mom to join us but she wants to stay in Nebraska. My dad disappeared a couple of decades ago, he went out for cigarettes and beer and never came back. My mom is under some delusion that someday he'll just randomly return as if nothing's ever happened. So, she won't leave."

"But… your sister—" Mariam interrupts.

I run my hand through my hair in frustration.

"Yeah, I know. I have more money than I could ever spend in a lifetime, my sister finds missing people for a living and my future brother-in-law works for a semi-clandestine law enforcement-type agency that can do who-knows-what, but my dad is still missing. Trust me, I see the irony in that. Someday, I'll sort out the mess that is my dad — but today's not that day."

Mariam lays her hand on my shoulder. "I'm sorry. I can't even imagine what that's like. I was a basket case when someone tried to kill my dad. They came way too close. I don't know what I would've done if they would have succeeded. Do you ever get to see your mom?"

"Occasionally. She's not a big fan of flying. I think she'll probably be out here for the holidays this year, though. Kendall has been pleading with her to come."

"I'm surprised you haven't pulled a stunt like Tristan and bought your own plane if you have all that money. You know, he and Aidan O'Brien are in some sort of weird competition over who can do the most nice things for their friends. Tristan runs some sort of unofficial air taxi service for everybody. If you want to fly your mom here by private jet, all you have to do is ask Tristan. I'm sure he would volunteer."

"I know it doesn't seem like it because I was working out of Kendall's basement, but according to my financial advisors, I can buy my mom a whole fleet of airplanes if I want to. I won't though because that would totally freak her out."

"Honestly, I get it. As much as you love your mom, planes don't exactly say, 'Happy Mother's Day'."

I chuckle. "I'm all about grand gestures, but even I agree a plane is a little much — but it's more than that. My mom isn't into technology. She still uses a television with rabbit ears. She can't tell one smartphone from another. It means nothing to her that I had the three largest phone makers fighting for the patent to my phone charger. My mom doesn't understand that I'm still working even though I don't put on a suit and go to an office from nine to five every day. She's never forgiven me for dropping out of college. I'm pretty sure she thinks I'm going to come back home any second and be begging for food."

Mariam rolls her eyes at me and groans. "Great! You're a college dropout too. You know, you're not helping your case here."

I abruptly stand up and stalk toward the other side of the office. I'm sure Mariam has no idea how many buttons she has pushed with her sarcasm. I take a deep breath and attempt to collect myself. "You never can tell. Paul Allen, Steve Jobs, and Michael Dell seemed to do just fine."

Mariam's eyes widen as she processes the anger I am unable to hide in my voice. "I'm sorry. That was uncalled for. I know people don't have to go to college to be successful — look at my brother. He dropped out too and he's fine."

With a sigh of relief, I walk back over to the leather couch and squat down beside her. "College isn't for everyone. But, it doesn't mean I'm a failure."

"I didn't mean to be rude. I'm just really scared all this is a pipe dream and too good to be true."

"Part of the reason I hired you is to make sure the dream stays true to my purpose. I'm finding that running the charity is more work than I expected. It's draining my creativity and hurting Hallway Innovations. I promise you there is real work to be done here. I can prove it to you. Are you ready to get started?"

I stand and reach down to take Mariam's hand to help her off the couch.

She reaches up to take my hand. As she stands, she says, "I guess I better start learning your business from the ground up." She stops to admire her desk and computer before she turns around. "What system do you use to keep your business records?"

I clear my throat and look at the ground. "You know that gut instinct which told you to turn down the job? You might want to revisit that feeling when you see my filing system," I confess.

Mariam takes off her jacket and folds the sleeves of her blouse up to her elbows. "I told you I'm tough and I don't quit easily. Besides, I worked as a teacher's assistant during graduate school. I've seen just about everything there is to see. How bad can it be?"

I flinch. "You might not want to ask that." I place my hand on the small of her back as I escort her back to a storage room.

Mariam waits silently as I turn the light on. "I don't see any filing cabinets," she finally ventures after I don't say anything.

"The paperwork is in those boxes."

A soft gasp escapes and she covers her mouth. "Those boxes? The ones large enough I could sleep in them?"

I nod.

"Oh I see, your records are in hanging files and you simply haven't purchased filing cabinets yet, right?"

I shake my head. "Sorry."

She draws in a deep breath before she asks hopefully, "Sorted by year, at least?"

I blush. "Approximately?"

"Is that a statement or a question?"

"Both?"

"Oh vey! Is it too early for me to ask for a raise?"

Looking over at the tall stack of enormous boxes, I realize what an overwhelming task I've asked of Mariam. I'm an "out of sight, out of mind" kind of guy. It's far too easy for me to focus on the things I like to do and ignore the things I hate.

"If you'll stay, you can name your price. As you can see, I desperately need your help. I wasn't kidding."

Anxiously, I wait as Mariam returns to the main office space and walks the circumference of the office in a slow circle stopping every few feet to look at the new equipment. Eventually, she makes her way back to where I'm standing. "I hope you're really as solvent as you say you are."

"That's what they tell me."

"You mean you don't know?"

"Presumably, that's what it says in these boxes. I trust the people around me."

"Please tell me you're exaggerating."

"Mariam, most of my people have been with me since I was eating white bread and mayonnaise sandwiches — and not because I like 'em."

"I know you want to believe people are honest — but that doesn't mean they are. Okay, it's clear you need me. But I can't do this by myself. You need to hire me an assistant. That wouldn't be a bad idea anyway considering my health issues."

"Okay, that seems reasonable. Anything else?"

"Yeah, I want you to hire Phoenix Wolf or Tobias Payne to come set up the system. We've got a lot of work to do and I want to make sure we do it as efficiently as possible. I don't want anything to fall through the cracks. Those guys are the smartest computer geeks I know."

"What about Jameson?" I ask, referring to my future brother-in-law.

"Jameson is smart, but he's better suited to catching bad guys. Unless your accountants are criminals, I think Toby's skills will be plenty."

"You drive a hard bargain, but I hired you to make sure my charity is run as efficiently as it can be. I have no doubt that's exactly what you'll do. Welcome to Hallway Innovations."

Chapter Eight

Mariam

It's all I can do not to drum my fingers on the desk as I wait for the software to finish installing. I look up at Toby as I try to keep my panic at bay. "Do you think all of this will help? This is years' worth of work. I don't even know what all of this paperwork is."

Toby looks around the office. "We all have our talents. It's clear Will's isn't paperwork or organization. Don't worry, this office automation will help."

"I think I'll need a little more than a few computers to fix this mess."

"Didn't Will give you permission to hire whoever you needed?"

I nod. "We talked about it. I think I've decided to hire a data entry person and someone to assist me with the organization. I don't know if you've heard but I have fibro. I can't spend forever typing on the computer or I won't be of any use to anyone. Will says that's fine. Now, I have to fill the positions. It ought to be interesting to tell them I don't know the scope or the complexity of the job and hope they're willing to come along for the adventure."

"As far as data entry goes, I don't know anyone off-hand but I could ask around."

"And the other position?"

Toby looks around, fidgets and avoids my gaze. "I don't know if I should even mention this, it's a big ask."

I gesture around the office. "Nothing about this job is normal. I landed it in the back of a limo when I didn't even know I was having a real job interview. Whatever it is, spit it out."

"Well, I know somebody who would be awesome for a job like this. She learns quickly, and she has a creative vibe which would work well with Will's style."

"But?" I prompt.

"She's got a lot of family drama. So much so she had to become emancipated. You know my story, right?"

"Bits and pieces," I admit.

"Well, you know I was taken and bad things happened to me as a teenager."

"I heard."

"Something similar happened to my friend. She wasn't gone nearly as long as me, but she'd like to get away from her hometown and the memories on the East Coast. She's young — not quite eighteen. She has a GED. She works incredibly hard, and she is a survivor."

"Do you think she'd even want to work here? She would be sorting papers. It's not exactly a stimulating job."

"Nothing personal, Ms. Fischer — but Isadora would shovel horse manure if it meant she could get a fresh start."

"You said she would be relocating. Where would she stay?"

Toby blushes bright red. "I haven't thought that far ahead. Even though we're friends, I don't think she'd feel comfortable staying with me."

"Let me talk to Will and see if it's something he'd be interested in. I doubt he'll have a problem. It seems consistent with his overall mission. If he agrees, I could offer Isadora a room at my place. My townhouse has been pretty empty since Elijah and Mindy got their own place."

The corner of Toby's mouth hitches up. "Wouldn't it be something if Will's paperwork aversion turns out to be the miracle that makes everyone else's dreams come true?"

"That would be something all right," I answer with a tired sigh as I consider the gigantic task in front of me.

"Like Mindy says, 'Sometimes the best answer requires the most work'."

I blow my hair out of my face as I let out a frustrated breath. "Can I tell you how much I hate it when my sister-in-law talks like a fortune cookie?"

Toby shrugs. "Yeah, I know. But that doesn't necessarily mean Mindy is wrong."

— • —

"I love it here and I don't mean to be disrespectful,

but…" the young Latina says as she scoops another huge stack of papers deep from within a box in the middle of a pile of boxes in our office. "… maybe Mr. K should be nominated for one of those hoarding shows."

I raise an eyebrow. "Yeah? What makes you say that, Isadora?"

"I sorted a pile of papers this morning. You'll never guess all the random stuff I found in it. He had tax papers from eight years ago, tickets to see the Cleveland Cavaliers — unused ones! — and four takeout menus for pizza places in Nebraska."

"Sounds like the pile I sorted the other day. It had his report card from third grade, last year's taxes, and Kendall's homecoming picture."

"Okay, this is a dumb question, but why are we sorting through all this stuff? Obviously, computers generated most of it, so where are those files?"

I stretch out my back as I stand and survey the office. "Good question. I haven't had the chance to ask Will because he's been out of town. Toby just finished setting up the network yesterday. All of our computers should be online now."

Isadora blanches. "Will I have to use the computers much? I've been avoiding social media since 'The Incident'."

"The Incident." It still blows me away that she's able to calmly refer to the months of her life that were stolen from her when she was kidnapped, raped, psychologically tortured and made to handle responsibilities no teenager should ever face. Most of the time, she does a good job of hiding behind the façade of a happy, carefree teenager excited about her new adventure in the Pacific Northwest. Moments like this remind me that all is not right in her world.

"Izzy, don't worry about it. There's enough stuff to do around here that if you don't want to use social media, there is no reason you need to."

She flops down in one of the spinning office chairs with the type of grace only teenagers possess. "This really sucks! I used to be great at it too. I could have done lots for Mr. K's charity. But now, every time I turn the computer on, I feel like I want to throw up."

I walk over and kneel in front of her as she wipes tears from her cheeks. "The cool thing about working here is that we're all kind of making up the rules as we go along. Will is really flexible. You're not the only one who is working around challenges. There will be days my disability will make it impossible for me to work."

"What disability? You don't look disabled," Isadora responds with a confused expression.

"Not everyone with a disability is like Kiera or Maddie. You can't always tell. I have fibromyalgia."

"What does that mean? I've never heard of it."

"That's a good question. The doctors don't even agree about what it means. But, most doctors think it's caused by a miscommunication between the signals in my brain and my nerves. It causes all sorts of different symptoms. Sometimes my life is relatively normal; but other times, I have extreme pain and fatigue. It can get so bad that even someone brushing up against me is painful. I think the worst symptom is the mental fog that comes with it."

"Oh, that sounds awful. Can't they give you a pill or

something to make you better?"

"I take some antidepressants and anti-inflammatories to help with the nerve pain, but there really is no cure."

"Wow! That sounds like me. They said I have post-traumatic stress disorder from what happened to me. I'm on all sorts of meds but my counselor says the best thing I can do to help myself is to avoid things that trigger me. Well … easy for her to say. She doesn't have to function with my brain now."

I want to cry for Izzy. I've had those same thoughts so many times, I can't even tell you.

Before I can say anything, she continues, "That's part of the reason I moved. My friends and family expected me to be the same person I was before. But that's never, ever going to happen. Something in me changed … forever. Like I said, looking at a computer makes me queasy. I went back to an old school flip phone. You know, the kind my parents used to carry? I might have to push the number 7 four times to get the S to be able to send a text message, but it'll be a lot harder for some weird pedophile to track me down. But, there is no way I could ever avoid all my triggers. It's impossible. I don't even know what they all are."

"I understand. I never know what will cause me to have a flare either. I can guess based on when it's happened before, but other times it seems random. So, we'll do our best to help each other, okay? For now, would it help you if I set up your computer as just a workstation, free of any external connection to the Internet? I'm sure Toby could do that for us."

Izzy nods. "Yeah, I think that would help a lot. I

know they arrested the guy who kidnapped me, but I still can't help the feeling he can see everything I do."

"I don't blame you. If you ever feel uncomfortable here, let me know and we'll do what we can to make it easier."

The back door suddenly opens and Isadora and I jump. She cowers behind a desk. I pull a can of mace out of my pocket. Will comes around the corner with a box of pizza and a six-pack of soda. He is grinning, but when he sees Izzy and what's in my hand, his expression quickly sobers.

He sets the food down on my desk and studies my expression. "Whoa! What did I miss?"

Izzy stands up and wipes her hands on the thighs of her jeans. "Sorry about that, Mr. K. Weird things set me off now. I didn't know you were coming. Could you do me a favor and come in the front door if you're going to surprise us?"

"Of course." Will looks over his shoulder at me. "Order me another door chime for the back door too. I didn't even think about how quiet it would be in here."

"How did your trip go, Mr. K?"

"I'm still not a fan of flying, even if I get to do it first class these days. Still, I got a lot of stuff accomplished. How did things go around here?"

"Maybe I shouldn't say anything." Isadora giggles and then covers her mouth.

"Go ahead, I never punish people for telling me the truth," Will says as he grabs a napkin and a piece of pizza. "Lay it on me."

Izzy gestures around the room where we tried to

sort things into a semblance of order. "Umm … you're not very organized for a grown-up. We were going to ask you if maybe your accountants or whoever you get this financial information from have computer files."

"I can't argue with the truth. I'm a lot of things. I'm a genius when it comes to designing things, I'm a below average cook, I am a sharp dresser and animals love me. But, you're right. Organizing things and keeping my room clean — not my favorite thing to do."

"Seriously? That's what you're going to stick with?" I answer with a smirk. "You have a business to run here. You're not a recalcitrant teenager."

Will sighs. "I brought you guys pizza and everything."

Izzy walks over and grabs a slice. "My favorite kind too." She takes a bite and then walks over to her desk and sits down. "Mr. K, we're not trying to rag on you, we're just trying to help you."

Will raises an eyebrow and gestures toward the stack of boxes. "I may be too far gone. I'm not sure you guys can do much at this point."

"Before everything went crazy in my life, I was taking a business applications class at my school. My teacher, Mrs. Ellison, told me I was really good. She was teaching us how to use some accounting software. If I had your information, I could help you keep track of expenses and all that stuff. So, do you have those files?"

Will hangs his head. "I should, shouldn't I?" He takes in a deep breath and lets it out. "I know you guys probably think I'm a terrible boss but I don't track details very well. I let other people take care of it and tell me what's going on."

Izzy's jaw drops open. "And you just believe them? Holy cow! I didn't even let my parents keep track of my allowance. I wrote it all down. Don't you have like millions and millions of dollars?" She pauses for a moment. "Wait a minute — are you like Mariam?"

Will's eyes cut sharply to mine. I meet his gaze and shrug. "What do you mean?"

"Well, Mariam was explaining that she has a disability nobody can see. I wondered if you do too. You remind me of my little brother. Pablo has a tough time in school because he's hyper. He hates any kind of homework."

Will takes a drink of his soda with excruciating slowness. As the silence drags on, Izzy looks at me with a crushed expression. Finally, she blurts, "I'm sorry, I shouldn't have said anything. If you're going to fire me, can you give me a few days to find something else? I don't want to move back home."

Will looks startled by her comment. "Iz, why would you think I'd fire you over a question like that?"

"Umm… 'cause it was kind of rude," Isadora admits.

Will chuckles softly. "Mariam here can tell you I specialize in sticking my foot in my mouth. I won't fire you for something like that. Turns out you're correct. I was well known among my teachers."

"Let me guess — you liked to hog the spotlight back then too?" I tease.

He leans forward and rests his elbows on his knees and rubs his temples. "Not exactly. I guess you could say Kendall and I were like two sides of the coin."

"Who is Kendall?" Izzy asks.

"She's my twin sister. She was good, and I was bad."

I draw in a sharp breath. "I'm sure that's not true. My friends adore you and, like Heather said, they're picky. They don't like bad people."

"Okay, I'm not really bad. But that's how it felt when I was a kid. Kendall breezed through school. The teachers always commented on how much they wanted or needed me to be more like my sister. But I couldn't pull myself together. None of the teachers' instructions made sense and I couldn't hold still in class and I didn't seem to learn like the rest of the kids. My brain was in a completely different space. I was always thinking about tearing things apart and putting them back together to make something else. I didn't care about English, math, or history."

"I bet you were one of those kids who lived for recess," I remark.

"Surprisingly, no. I didn't really get along with the other kids very well. They all thought I was weird. It got even worse after my dad disappeared."

Izzy's eyes are as big as saucers as she watches Will tell his story. "Your dad was kidnapped too? That's just too weird!"

Will shakes his head. "No, as far as we know, he just left. He was never the same after he came back from the war. He told my mom he was going to the store. He decided not to come home."

Isadora pops to her feet and sprints over to stand right in front of Will's face. "How do you know? You don't! He could be locked away in some dingy basement somewhere. Have you even looked for him? You should have Toby or Officer Erickson or somebody look for him!" Izzy's voice breaks with tears. "What if no one had ever looked for me?"

Will stands up and gathers her in a hug. "Izzy, calm down. I'm already on it. While I was on my trip, I stopped by to visit with my mom and I got some more information to help Tristan, Jameson, Toby, or all of them look for my dad."

Izzy pulls away and returns to her desk. "How did you know I would freak out about it?"

"I didn't. But I have a bunch of stuff I need to get figured out. One of them is my relationship with my dad."

"What if it's too late?" Izzy asks softly.

"To be honest, I sort of figure it already is. I hope I'm wrong, but you know—"

"Maybe he's okay. You never know. I didn't mean to make you sad, I just wanted to ask you about some computer files," Izzy replies.

"Look, we're all going to be working together and as you can see, life can get a little messy. And you should probably know life with me will probably be messier than most. You were right. I had a learning disability — I figured I'd outgrown it. When I was younger, they put me through all sorts of testing to figure out what was wrong with me. The best thing they could come up with is that my brain doesn't process information the way everyone else does."

"So you have Asperger's like Phoenix?" I ask.

"Not exactly. I'm not on the autism spectrum — or at least they didn't think so when I was in school. I just seem to see and hear information differently. One of the doctors said it was like auditory processing disorder.

So, it was just easier for me to figure out things on my own than to read or listen to instructions."

Izzy's face lights up. "I get it. The thing that makes you great at inventing things makes you terrible at being a normal business person."

"That about sums it up," Will answers with a self-deprecating smile.

Izzy grins back. "Well, it's a really good thing you hired us. We are going to turn Hallway Innovations around and make you look like a respected titan of business."

Will walks over to Isadora and gives her a high five. "If you guys can do that, I'll have to do better than pizza."

"Counting on it, Boss!"

CHAPTER NINE

WILL

MARIAM NERVOUSLY PLACES THE napkin over her lap as the waiter pours her some ice water and places some steaming coffee in front of me. After he leaves, she looks up and gathers the courage to ask, "Okay, I've engaged in about as much polite chitchat as I've got in me. Can you tell me why we're here and not at the office? I hate to sound like Izzy, but did you invite me here to fire me?"

I choke on the coffee I was sipping. "I'm not sure how I got a reputation as a tyrant. Have I really been so bad?"

Mariam blushes. "No, you've been more than patient with us. It's hard for us to trust people, given what we've been through recently. Isadora and I are a little skittish. Try not to take it personally."

"But, you're happy at Hallway Innovations, right?"

She nods enthusiastically. "It wasn't anything like I expected, but I think we're both settling in okay. I like working with Isadora. I'm glad she found a place to stay with Kiera and Jeff. I would've taken her in, but I think Toby had a point. It might've been awkward for her to stay with me and for me to be her boss too."

"I get the feeling Jeff misses having Mindy around since she got married."

"Izzy tells me she and Becca have become good friends and she's starting to feel more like a normal teenager. I guess Becca is talking to her about going on college visitation trips."

I raise an eyebrow. "Really? That would be totally cool! Maybe I need to set up a new college scholarship program for employees of Hallway Innovations. I don't want Izzy to have to worry about financing school."

Mariam looks puzzled. "I could've sworn you were anti-college."

"Oh, never! It simply wasn't the best option for me. I was so proud of Kendall when she graduated."

The corner of Mariam's mouth hitches up. "Hmm, if you want to make your college tuition program retroactive, it wouldn't hurt my feelings. I am going to be buried in debt from my school loans until I'm old enough to collect Social Security."

I grin. "Let's make a deal. For every year you work for Hallway Innovations, I'll pay for a year of your student loans until they're all paid off."

Mariam's jaw goes slack. "Do you have any idea how much money that is? I went to graduate school. The cost of my textbooks for a single term was like half my rent for the townhouse."

"I know. Kendall used to complain about that kind of stuff all the time while she was getting her master's degree. I can handle it."

Her brows furrow. "I'm not trying to sound ungrateful, but Izzy and I are still trying to get all the information imported into the right programs to make sure everything is on the up and up. I know you trust your financial people, but I'll feel better about things after we've confirmed it for sure. Your record-keeping habits are a disaster. There's no way you could know anything for certain."

I shrug. "Well, I figure it's a good thing I've never been audited by Uncle Sam. That has to be good news, right?"

"Good news or sheer luck. I'm not an accountant, but I understand they only audit a certain percentage of tax returns. You could just be incredibly lucky."

"Or my people could be honest. Maybe you're looking at the situation through jaded lenses."

"Trust me, I would love to be wrong. Nothing would make me happier. So, I know paperwork isn't your thing, but what do you think of what Izzy and I have done?"

I look down and fiddle with the sugar packet in front of me for a moment. "It's awesome…"

Mariam picks up on my hesitation. "But?"

"This whole experience has made me face some hard truths about myself."

"Oh, you mean your hoarding tendencies?"

I flinch. She wasn't kidding about being blunt. "Worse things have been said about me. But it's more than that. It was actually your honesty which started me on the right path."

"My honesty?" Mariam responds, her voice raising

to a surprised squeak. "When exactly? The first time we met — when I called you a shallow, rich jerk? Or maybe the second time when I accused you of stalking me? Or maybe it was after that when I called you a lazy slob?"

I wince. "Okay, I acknowledge we didn't get off to the best start. But you were also profoundly brave after the reception at Phoenix and Zoe's wedding. You didn't have to tell me about your challenges with fibro. I knew nothing about spoons and what it's like to fight your own body like that. I admire your courage."

Mariam sighs. "I don't want to be inspirational. I'd give anything for my life to go back to normal."

"I get it."

"How could you possibly?" Mariam snaps as she slaps the menu down on the table. "You skate through life and everything always works out for you."

"Actually, that's what working around you and Isadora has shown me. I thought I was skating by and fooling people. I was hiding behind this mask of being a kooky inventor guy who was eccentric because I chose to be. I could be as weird as I wanted to be because my brain operated on a different plane than everyone else. After all, I thought of things no one else thought of. I couldn't be bothered with average every-day concerns. If I dressed and acted the part, no one would know what I was hiding."

Mariam chews on her bottom lip for a moment while she puzzles through what I just said. "Hiding? I'm not sure I understand."

I scrub my hand down my face and take a deep breath and let it out before I say out loud what I've never admitted to another person before. "I'm still that little kid who doesn't understand the instructions. Only instead of a math test, these days, it's business contracts, rental agreements and taxes."

I wait for the earth to crumble around me, but Mariam merely nods. "That must be incredibly frustrating."

Her reaction ticks me off. "How can you be so calm? This will change my whole life. I thought all those stupid tests they had me take when I was a kid was something I would easily outgrow. You know, something just to check off boxes for paperwork in school. I didn't realize it would affect me forever."

Mariam studies me for a few moments. "Are you mad at me because I brought your learning disability to your attention?"

The waiter brings us our food and quietly sets it in front of us. Our conversation is so intense, his presence seems intrusive; but I'm grateful for the distraction because it gives me a moment to sort out my thoughts.

"Maybe!" I blurt candidly. "Okay, that's not fair. I'm mad at myself for not being able to fix it. If I can invent things which have never been dreamed up before why can't I organize my own thoughts and life? Why can't I figure out simple things normal people do every single day if I'm so darn smart? How does that make any sense?"

"It seems like it would be easier to pretend everything is normal, right?"

"Well, yeah," I answer sarcastically.

"I learned this lesson the hard way. Illness or disability doesn't wait until it's properly labeled to impact your life. I've known you now for four months.

Whatever your issues are, they definitely impact your life whether you name them or not. However, you're right. Your disguise is disarmingly effective. Anyone who casually meets you would never see your struggles. Your brilliance and kindness hide them well. Add a little chutzpah, charm, and good looks and your mask is complete. Those who don't know you don't know to look any deeper."

I take a bite of my filet mignon. Usually, it is my favorite dish here, but now it might as well be sawdust and chewing gum for as much trouble as I'm having chewing and swallowing my bite. I gulp a swig of my coffee which is now getting cold. "Truthfully, you and Izzy are the only people besides Kendall who I have let close enough to see that side of me. I don't know what I'm going to do. I can't live with Kendall the rest of my life and you guys aren't going to work with me forever." Much to my chagrin, my voice breaks with emotion.

"If you're anything like me or my other friends who've been through something similar, once you figure out what's happening to you — whether you read an article that rings a bell or you get a formal diagnosis from your doctor — your head will spin. You'll go back over everything in your life and try to make it make sense. You'll start kicking yourself and second-guessing decisions you've made in the past, wondering if you should have done something sooner or different to figure it out faster or prevent it from happening. One second you'll be thrilled you figured it out and the next second will be angry at the world. You'll be screaming 'why me?' and then laugh at your own arrogance and ask, 'why the heck not me?'"

"I knew Mindy could read minds, but I didn't know

you could too."

"Oh, there's no mind reading involved. I've just been there, done that, and earned the T-shirt, remember?"

"Okay, so what's next?"

"I highly recommend skipping this next step. It is rarely helpful. But everyone seems to do it anyway, so you might as well just do it and get it over with."

Mariam delicately slices her chicken marsala and takes a bite.

"Oh, I can't wait to hear this."

"Well, the natural tendency is to look up your diagnosis on the Internet and figure out all the latest treatments. Trust me, this is a rabbit hole you don't want to go down. If you get conflicting information, the next logical step is to ask your friends what they've heard about your disability. This opens a whole new can of worms. Everybody and their pet ferret will have an opinion about your disability."

"Great! What am I supposed to do? What I'm doing obviously isn't working. Otherwise, you and Izzy wouldn't be working overtime trying to make order out of absolute chaos and I wouldn't be living in my sister's basement."

"You need to find yourself a team. It can include your family, but it doesn't have to. This team has to be made up of people you trust — people you trust to see behind your mask. You need some medical professionals on this team who will give you information you believe. After you have that information, the other members of your team can develop a strategy with you to help you cope."

"You act like I was in a car accident or something. Nobody will take what I have seriously. As far as I know, nobody really knows what it is for sure."

Mariam scowls at me. "Haven't you learned anything from Izzy and me over the last few months? Just because you can't see the problem, doesn't mean it's not there. It's the nature of invisible disabilities."

"So you're saying you and Kendall are on my team by default?"

"Seems that way."

I make a show of wiping sweat off my forehead. "Boy, am I sure glad to hear that."

Mariam gives me a wary look over her glass of water. "Yeah, why do you say that?"

"You wouldn't leave your teammate in a lurch, would you?"

"Hmm ..." she responds noncommittally. "What's up?"

"Well, it seems the wedding bug was contagious. Kendall and Jameson have decided to tie the knot. They want to fly my mom out at Christmas."

"Oh, that'll be beautiful! I love Christmas weddings."

"You know, I'm a twin. That means Kendall expects me to be in the wedding ... as in the best man."

"I've seen you dressed up. You will be very handsome."

"M-Mariam ... I don't think you understand," I stammer awkwardly. "If I'm the best man, I need you to be the maid of honor."

"I'm sure Kendall has several close friends who would be more than honored to go down the aisle with you."

I shake my head. "She doesn't. Brynley is walking with Toby. Please, this is why I invited you out tonight because this isn't work related. I'm asking you as my friend. I don't want to let my sister down."

Mariam looks at me skeptically. "I don't know, Will. The last wedding didn't go so well."

"I guess that depends on your perspective. The way I look at it, our date that wasn't actually a date turned out to be the best thing ever. It turned us from enemies to teammates. You can't ask for much more."

Mariam sets her fork down. "You are so lucky I believe in team sports."

Unable to contain my happiness, I stand up and walk around the table. I pull Mariam up to a standing position and gather her into a loose embrace. "There aren't enough thank yous in the world for all you've done for me tonight."

Mariam pulls away slightly and stands up on her tiptoes. She brushes a kiss across my cheek. "Don't mention it. I believe in you."

It's such a simple gesture and declaration, but it means the world to me. I never want to let her go.

CHAPTER TEN

MARIAM

KENDALL LEANS BACK IN her chair as she licks the frosting off of her fork. "Heather, I don't know how you expect me to choose. I think I'll tell Jameson I want to stay engaged forever. All these decisions suck."

Heather hands her a pen and a little note card. "That's what all my potential brides say. We're flexible at Joy and Tiers. Just let me know how many people you plan to have at your wedding and what you've budgeted for cake, I'll work around that."

"You're kidding, right? You've met my brother. He told me to ignore any discussion of the budget. I can have everything I want for my wedding."

I groan. "She's not kidding. Will has been showing us endless bridal websites at work. We'll be lucky if he doesn't fly David Tutera in to be your wedding planner. For someone who was reluctant to be your best man, he has embraced it fully."

Kendall rolls her eyes. "No kidding, Mariam! He is scaring me."

"I worked with David when I did a cake for one of Aidan's celebrity friends. He's actually a nice guy," Heather grins.

Kendall buries her head in her hands. "You're not helping! I do not want this to be a tabloid-worthy wedding. You know if it gets crazy big, Jameson will feel like he has to be on duty. I just want our wedding to be a fun get-together with my friends and family."

"Fun weddings are never a problem around here."

"Yeah, I've heard you guys are legendary for your get-togethers," Brynley adds. "What kind of cake does Jameson like?"

"He's not picky about food. He even likes Twinkies," Kendall wrinkles her nose.

"What about you?" Heather asks. "Anything pop for you?"

Kendall surveys the plates in front of her. "Everything! I loved everything. If I can't even choose a flavor, how in the world am I going to choose a design?"

"Do you trust me?" Heather asks with a mischievous grin.

Kendall looks around the bakery with all the elaborate cake displays. "I wouldn't be here if I didn't."

"With your permission, I'll design something suited to you and Jameson. You won't even have to think about it. You are getting married at Trevor and Madison's barn, right?"

Kendall squeaks with delight. "Really? You can do that? I don't have to make any decisions? Promise me you won't go crazy with the budget. I know Will says he doesn't have any concerns about money, but I worry about him."

"I promise I won't bankrupt Will. This'll be fun. It's been a while since a client has given me full creative license," Heather remarks as she walks over to give Kendall a hug. "Don't worry. I'll take care of you guys."

Kendall looks over at Brynley and me. "I wish someone would take away all the decisions I have to make about dresses. I have the fashion sense of a fruit fly."

I catch Heather's eye and she winks at me. I reach out and put my hand on Kendall's forearm. "Uh … I know somebody who can help you … especially if Will is playing the role of a fairy godfather."

"As long as I don't have to try on a million dresses before I find the right one, count me in," Kendall replies.

Brynley is watching our interaction as if it's a tennis match. "I'm not sure I understand everything you guys are talking about but I can tell it'll be awesome. Kendall, don't forget I promised you my cousins would videotape your wedding."

I grin. "See? We've got you covered. You can relax and simply be a blissful bride."

Kendall stops and takes a sip of iced tea. "I'm so stressed out, I forgot I'm supposed to be happy. Thank you for reminding me. No wonder my brother digs you so much."

I clear my throat. "Truth be told, I like your brother a lot more than I ever expected to."

I watch Will as he examines the designs on Jordan's walls. "I can't believe you volunteered to come on this mission. Are you sure you want to hang out here?"

He shrugs. "I've always liked fashion. It's a little like inventing things. Besides, Kendall and I pinch-hit for each other all the time. She and Brynley had to speak at an important conference. She was completely stressed out about leaving you in a lurch. I'm happy to help."

I stick my tongue out at him and tease, "Some guys will do anything to get out of paperwork."

For a brief second, his eyes darken. He shakes it off and grins. "Just taking one for the team. If there are side benefits that's not my fault."

Jordan walks around the corner and takes her earpiece out and sets it down on the counter with her cell phone. "Sorry about that. Cristiano and I were trying to coordinate our schedules. He's been covering a race out of town. I wanted to make sure he wasn't expecting me to pick him up at the airport tonight."

"Oh, I could come back another time," I offer.

"Nonsense, my husband already has another ride. I'm all yours. So, how can I help you?"

"That's a really good question. Kendall didn't give me much guidance on bridesmaids' dresses. She just told me to wear what makes me feel beautiful. It would've been easier if she would've fretted over every last detail."

Jordan winks at me. "Ah ... So you've been a bridesmaid before?"

I roll my eyes. "Since you're a fashion designer, I

should probably keep my mouth shut."

Jordan grabs a tape measure and laughs. "Oh honey, why do you think I started designing my own clothes?"

Will's eyes light up. "See? I told you Jordan was a lot like me."

Jordan shoots him a puzzled look.

"I mean you identify problems and try to solve them," Will hastens to explain.

Jordan nods. "That's exactly what I do. The problem we have right now is how to dress you for Kendall's wedding. So, the question of the day is what makes you feel beautiful?"

"Not much. I'm not like Kendall and Brynley. Kendall has gorgeous blonde hair. The medication I take has made a lot of my hair fall out and what's left is all different sorts of lengths as I try to grow it back out. Brynley is young and agile and there are days I move like I'm eighty. I'm afraid I'm the character who doesn't belong in a Disney princess movie."

Will snaps his head around to look at me. "You don't even know how wrong you are."

I raise an eyebrow at him.

Jordan sits beside me on the antique couch in the studio and puts her hand over mine. My eyes pause on the different skin tones on her hands. I try to cover my reaction.

"No, that's okay. It's hard to ignore. But it's part of me — a part of me I used to hate. I used to cover my vitiligo with makeup, even on my hands and feet."

I fight back tears. I can relate to the hate. There are so many days I hate every cell of my body. "So … what changed?"

"I found someone who helped me change my definition of beautiful," Jordan answers with a wistful smile.

Will clears his throat. "If I can stop being your boss for a little while and just be a guy who likes the heck out of you, I think I can help you answer the question about what makes you beautiful."

My eyes widen with shock and I stare at him blankly.

"You mind?" he presses.

I shake my head mutely.

He reaches out and tucks my hair behind my ear. "This hair you hate so much? I think it's magical. It's a lot like you: ever-changing, but always shiny and beautiful in different ways. The color highlights your gorgeous brown eyes."

"I wear it different ways because I can't control this mop! You're being far too generous. Most of the time I just throw it up in a ponytail; it's not like it's a huge fashion statement," I protest.

Will rolls his shoulder. "I love it when you wear your hair up. I'm a sucker for old Hollywood and you remind me of Audrey Hepburn." He turns to Jordan. "I don't know what you had planned, but Mariam would look stunning in a red dress. You have to be careful about material though. Her skin is very sensitive."

Jordan looks up from her clipboard where she's taking notes. "I agree, Mariam would look magnificent in red. It would be perfect for a Christmas wedding too."

My mind is racing as I try to sort out the conversation. I can't figure out if Will is flirting with me or simply being nice. Worse yet, I can't decide which I want it to be.

"What do you think?" Jordan prompts.

"I think lots of things, but none of them make a lot of sense right now," I answer candidly.

"Well, let's start with the color. Do you like red?" Jordan asks patiently.

"Oh, yes! I love red." I chew on my bottom lip in indecision. "But… I think it's a little bold for the bridesmaids' dresses. We don't want to overshadow Kendall. After all, this is her day."

"Kendall and Jameson are so in love, nothing will outshine them. Besides, I've started on Kendall's dress and it's a head turner. I wouldn't worry about it. Like she said, wear what makes you feel beautiful."

"What about Brynley and Mindy?" I stammer.

"Will is the best man and you are the maid of honor. So they want you to choose first," Jordan insists.

I glance over helplessly at Will. "Red? Are you sure?"

He nods. "I'm sure. It suits you perfectly."

"Really? Maybe it used to, but these days I'm not that bold."

Will stands up and moves in front of me. He gets down on his knees and grasps my hands. "That's just not true, Mariam. I've worked with you for months now. You're bold every single day."

"I am?" I whisper.

"You are. I watch you work through pain that would make most of us curl up and call our mamas for help. Yet, you don't complain. You even reached out to help someone else rise above her pain. That makes you out-of-this-world bold and more beautiful than any other woman I've ever met."

Jordan wipes away tears. "I don't care what you say. For this man, you should wear red because he sees who you really are."

"I'm not sure I know the person he sees," I reply.

Will squeezes my hands. "Then it's my job to introduce you to her. Once you get to know that Mariam, I think you'll be amazed."

CHAPTER ELEVEN

WILL

I HAVE TO STEP back as sparks fly and the smell of singed plastic fills my workshop. So much for that prototype. Crap! I had such high hopes for that one. I reach for my coffee and I'm a little confused when I find my cup empty. Geez, I need to get more sleep. I don't even remember drinking it.

Sleep. I vaguely remember the days when I could. These days, I don't get much. My mind is far too occupied with thoughts of Mariam to rest.

It's strange how one day can change everything yet change nothing at all. That day at Jordan's shop, I was just being honest when I told Mariam how I see her. It shouldn't have been a big deal. I thought she knew — it's not like I've been shy about how I feel. But somehow, that day, it was different.

Since my little confession, Mariam is a little wary around me. Outwardly, she's still polite but there's a distance that wasn't there before. In some ways, I wish I had said nothing at all, but in other ways, I'm glad I did. Mariam needs to be told every single day how strong and beautiful she is. I guess I don't regret what I said — but perhaps the way I said it.

My coffee cup isn't going to re-fill itself. I suppose I should stop hiding in my workshop and see how things are going up front. I turn on the fans to clear out the stench in the workshop and grab my cup off my workbench.

I pause at the end of the hallway to watch my business hum along. I wish those creeps in high school could see me now — especially the teacher who told me I was too stupid to graduate from high school, much less make anything of myself. Okay, Hallway Innovations isn't Microsoft or Apple, but we're making a difference in the world and I'm okay with that.

"Mariam is on the other line, but I'll be sure to let her know you called, Jaxson," Isadora says cheerfully as she writes on a message pad.

Mariam is scowling at the computer. "That's the formula I have in the F13 cell. Are you sure I didn't import the information incorrectly? Yes, I double checked it against the hard copy. Okay, I just wanted to be certain. Thanks for being a second set of eyes." Mariam sets down the phone and rubs her temples.

I stroll over to the coffee machine. "Hello ladies. How are things?" I remark casually as if I haven't been eavesdropping. "You guys want to go to lunch?"

Mariam groans. "I can't. I have to figure out what's going on."

Before I can say anything, Isadora shakes her head. "I have to come up with a polite way for the foundation to say 'no' so the Heywoods will stop calling me."

I walk over to Isadora's computer and glance at the

screen. "Who are we turning down?"

"I don't know if you're going to actually turn Robert Heywood down. I'm just gathering information for you," Isadora quickly backpedals.

"Okay, let me rephrase my question. Why are you drafting a rejection letter for me?"

Mariam glances up at the clock. "Let me put the closed sign up and we can move this staff meeting to the conference room."

"Staff meeting? I just asked Izzy a question."

"Trust me, the explanation requires a staff meeting."

I turn to Izzy and raise an eyebrow. "True?"

She nods. "There's a reason I have files with sticky notes and draft documents."

I cringe. "This was a lot easier when I chose my charity projects by throwing a dart."

Mariam shakes her head and rolls her eyes at me.

"I'm kidding — mostly. I only resorted to the dartboard if I couldn't decide between tough cases."

She chokes back an exasperated laugh. "I should be surprised, yet somehow I'm not." We all sit down at a large table made from reclaimed wood from an old barn. "But, these days you have a process in place — a process Shayna Heywood is not happy about. Izzy and I have heard from her nearly every day since we put it in place four months ago."

"She's applying for free money from the Heart Wish Foundation, how could she have a problem with us?"

"I'm not exactly sure, but she most definitely does," Mariam explains with a sour expression.

"So, remember when I developed the website and the form with Toby?"

"Yeah, I thought it was a great idea to standardize the application process, require medical documentation, and get reference letters."

Isadora leans forward and slides an application toward me. "Shayna Heywood was crazy-mad that we made her fill out an application. I thought her reaction was so cray-cray, I did some more digging."

"Crazy how?"

Izzy shrugs. "You told me to trust my gut if something felt off in this job. This lady was sending up smoke signals everywhere I looked. First, she swore up and down that her friend got help from HWF before without having to provide any information."

"Well, I guess technically that's possible. Although I did ask at least a few questions before I just handed out money," I answer as I turn a deep shade of red.

Izzy shakes her head. "But get this — she couldn't even name her friend. The hair on the back of my neck stood up."

"Mariam, you spoke to this woman, what do you think?"

She clears her throat. "As you know, every request Heart Wish gets is unique. But most families are just grateful for any bit of help. This lady is different. She's not asking so much as demanding. She makes me grind my teeth."

"Yeah, the woman is mega rude. I haven't talked to

Robert much but what little I did … was weird."

"What do you mean?"

"Honestly, that's what made me dig a little deeper. They submitted an incredibly touching video that showed Robert in a wheelchair. He allegedly has some sort of very rare neurological condition that only a handful of people in the whole world have. In the video, he could barely move his mouth to speak. His words were slurred, and it was difficult to understand what he was saying. One day I called Shayna to confirm I had received a fax from her doctor's office and Robert answered the phone. I was totally weirded out since his mom told me he couldn't talk anymore. But he sounded like any teenager just like me. He didn't sound sick at all."

"Wow! That's an interesting plot twist."

"So, that's not all —"

"But, what if his disability is like yours and the effects come and go?" I interrupt, as I glance over to Mariam.

"We thought about that. That's why we asked Jaxson to double check for us. Doctor Shepherd asked one of his colleagues who specializes in neurology. If Robert Heywood has what they claim he has, his symptoms would get progressively worse, but they would never get better."

"Maybe he was having a bad day on the day they made the video," I argue, unwilling to believe the worst.

"Mr. K, I'm sorry, but I found this on YouTube," Isadora pushes her iPad toward me.

"Wait! What? I thought you didn't do social media."

Isadora smiles awkwardly. "I didn't for a while. But Toby's been helping me face down my demons. I figured I needed to deal with it for my job and it turned out to be super important. Just watch —"

For several minutes I silently watch a video of a bunch of teenage boys riding skateboards in front of what looks like an office complex. It's not hard to pick out Robert Heywood with his bright red hair and freckles. After one particularly complex trick, he comes right up to the camera and says, "Dude! Did you see that? I totally nailed it. Take that, all you haters. I told you I could! I, Robert Shane Heywood, rule the boarding universe!"

I blink several times as I wait for my brain to process what I just saw. "Maybe this was posted before he got sick," I grasp at straws.

Mariam stands up and comes over to put her arm around my shoulders. "No, we had Toby check that too. The video was posted three weeks after we received the application."

"There's no chance his illness is cyclical?" I confirm.

Beside me, I feel Mariam shake her head. "It isn't. Shayna Heywood represented that her son was close to dying. The medical evidence that we requested doesn't even come close to backing that up."

"So what's wrong with Robert Heywood?" I ask still trying to wrap my brain around this.

"Doctor Shepherd says aside from some panic attacks and asthma, the main thing that's wrong with him is his mom," Isadora answers with a haunted expression.

"Mariam, you said you were working on something too. Do we need to discuss it?"

She shakes her head. "No, I think we've dealt with enough for now. My issue can wait. I changed my mind — we need a lunch date after all. I could use a healthy dose of chocolate."

"I agree. I might need French fries to deal with this day," Izzy adds.

<hr>

"Thanks for letting me come over and vent." I set down a bag of sandwiches from the deli.

"No problem," Mariam says as she tucks her hands in the pockets of her oversized sweatshirt. "It was quite a day."

I glance around the townhouse with the marble fireplace. "Nice place you have here."

"Wish I could take credit for it, but Elijah got this after Dad was hurt. After he got married, I loved it so much I couldn't bear to move out. Thanks to the job at Hallway Innovations, I'm able to stay here. I'm sorry I was so skeptical at first. Have I ever told you how much I like working for you?"

I hang my head in frustration. "Even on days like today? Can you believe this garbage? Who lies to a charity? I don't have to give these people my money!"

Mariam runs her hand down my cheek. "I'm so sorry, Will. I don't know why people lie. I wish I had an easy answer. My dad was almost killed because people thought it was easier to lie to get ahead than to work hard."

"But this woman used a child! How sick is she? Do you think he knows what's going on?"

Grimacing, she nods. "He has to. He starred in the application video. Robert was sitting in a custom glammed out wheelchair pretending not to be able to move or speak and then a couple weeks later he was out skateboarding with his friends. He has to be in on it."

"That's beyond disgusting. Spreading your lowlife tendencies to another generation like it's nothing —"

"I know. It makes me nauseous. We get so many requests for help from people who can't even afford their next mortgage payment and then to get something like this is mind-boggling."

"What were they asking for again?"

"You mean demanding? The family demanded that HWF provide their allegedly dying child with tickets to an elite gaming conference over in Europe complete with backstage passes to meet the celebrity gamers and first-class tickets for their whole extended family."

I chuckle. "Oh, is that all? Even with my connections to Tristan, I haven't scored backstage passes."

"That's not all. They wanted a new gaming system for him so he could play all the games and become proficient at them before the event. They also demanded a new vehicle so they could get to the airport. I tell you, Shayna Heywood is a piece of work. Izzy told me her kidnapper was a lot more reasonable than this chick."

"Well, it's probably a good thing Izzy is the one drafting the denial letter. Because if it were up to me, my letter would be a string of profanities followed by the phrase 'hell-to-the-no'."

Mariam chuckles. "To be honest, I think that's what Isadora is struggling with. Her first couple of drafts sounded a lot like yours."

"As they should! What kind of idiot does she think I am?"

"I don't know. I don't think we're the idiots here. She's probably tried this before and gotten away with it. It's the only way her anger makes any sense. If we were her first marks, she would've simply scratched us off the list and moved on down. She wasn't expecting to run into analytical brains and the princesses of skepticism."

I grin. "'Princesses of Skepticism'. I like that. I might have some business cards made up with that title. You know, I'm tempted to play along with this kid's scheme. It wouldn't be so hard to call Tristan in Florida and ask him for one of the games his programmers have scrapped. I could make Robert think he was getting a chance to hang out with the gaming elite."

"Will —" Mariam tries to interrupt.

"No, listen … we could fly 'em somewhere on Tristan's plane and make Ms. Fancy pants I-have-to-fly-first-class feel like she's won the lottery and then lose the wheelchair in front of a bunch of cameras. We could expose them for the scam artists they are."

Mariam takes a bite out of her sandwich. When she is finished, she gives me a steely stare. "Or not. I know you're hurt by their lies. At some point, they'll get caught, but making a spectacle out of them will only hurt your credibility. Is that what you want the Heart Wish Foundation to be known for? We're not some tabloid TV show. People come to us when they are at their most vulnerable. We want them to trust us to help them. We are not in the business of getting even."

I sigh and lean back against Mariam's couch. "You know they'll just keep doing this?"

"Probably. But like you said, you don't have to give them money. There are so many deserving people we can focus on. Eventually, they'll mess up. I'm guessing sooner rather than later. Shayna's mouth will probably catch up with her."

"Can I at least speed the process along? I could put some choice words in the denial letter."

"Hey, you're the boss. You can do whatever you want, but I don't recommend it."

"Doesn't this tick you off?" I demand. "Their lies are stealing money from people who actually deserve it. How can you be so philosophical about it all?"

Mariam sets her sandwich down and takes a long drink of her iced tea. She settles back on the couch and crosses one leg under the other. "There isn't much I hate on the planet more than liars."

"Then how can you be so calm?"

"I'm not. I just don't have the energy to fight them anymore. Liars have changed who I am as a person. I'm tired of giving them that power."

"What do you mean changed you?"

"This is a long story, are you sure you want to hear it?"

"Venting goes both ways."

"This is old hurt. I don't think about it much anymore except on days like today when I'm reminded people like Ralph can be remarkably scummy."

"Who is Ralph?"

"My old high school boyfriend — although he preferred to be called Ray. My parents wanted me to stay around Oregon to go to school but I wanted to follow Ralph. So off to Chicago we went. Everybody told us we were too young to be serious. But I knew better. We were going to be one of those old-fashioned couples who made it work, regardless of the odds."

"I know what you mean. My grandparents were like that."

"So, off we went, halfway across the United States to go to school. I was so excited. I had a guy who told me he loved me to the moon and back. He was handsome and smart and I had my whole life ahead of me. What could possibly go wrong?"

"On a college campus? The possibilities boggle the mind." I smirk. "Of course, you're talking to the guy who dropped out after a couple of terms."

"Perhaps I should've quit, but I was too blasted stubborn."

"So what happened between you and lover boy?"

"At first, it was fine. I was the kind of girlfriend he wanted. I went to all the games and parties with him and looked suitably pretty. 'Ray' played basketball. He loved being a popular jock. Ralph, the shy kid with braces I tutored in English in the seventh grade was long gone. Ralph was a wonderful, sensitive artist. We were planning to open a gallery with a studio where we could paint together when we graduated from college."

"A gallery? I had no idea you even enjoyed painting."

"I don't … anymore."

"What? That would be like turning off the part of me that invents things."

"Like I said, Ralph's lies wrote on the soul of me and changed who I am as a person."

"What did he do to you? You're like, the strongest person I know."

"I am now, but I wasn't always. I learned the hard way. Ralph and others like him made me tough."

My body tenses as I sit up. "What do I need to do to the jerk?"

"Nothing. I've decided to let karma deal with the likes of him."

"What did he do?"

"Well, like I said, at first things were fine. But then I started getting sick. At first, the doctors thought I had mono. But I didn't. Then they thought it was Lyme disease. It didn't turn out to be that either. I kept going to the doctor trying to figure out what was wrong with me and Ralph got really frustrated with me because I didn't feel well enough to party with his friends or help him with his homework."

"If you were sick, why wasn't he helping you?" I ask indignantly.

"That's a good question. He kept telling me he was too busy with sports and his friends to deal with me. I fell behind in my classes and was at risk of losing my scholarship but Ralph didn't care. He only cared that I looked the part of the perfect girlfriend. So, when he told me he loved me and wanted to be with me forever, he only meant if I was perfect. Once I wasn't perfect, I was invisible to him. So, I don't know if that makes him the world's biggest liar or me the biggest fool."

"Without a doubt, he was the fool. But how did he change your dreams?"

"Like an idiot, I signed up for every class with him. After we broke up, he and his friends were laughing at me every time I went to class. So, I went to an advisor and completely changed my schedule. I avoided all the art classes I adored and took anything else available on the schedule. I ended up taking weird classes like statistics and epidemiology. Much to my surprise, I was actually good at them. I guess I have my dad's engineering brain after all."

"But you don't paint at all now?"

Mariam shakes her head. "No, I can't. It's like that part of me was destroyed by the pain. I don't know if it's the pain from the fibro or the devastation from the breakup or what exactly — it's as if my soul decided I'm no longer an artist."

"Wow! It doesn't sound like you're so 'over it' after all."

Mariam shrugs. "You could be right. But there's not a lot I can do about it. The person I was back then is long gone. I've learned my lesson. People who say they love me for me don't know what they're up against. The me who is here today might be gone tomorrow. A skill I have today may evaporate like a fine mist."

"I hate that one person had that much power over you."

"Will, it was way more than just one person. It was one person and a disease that no one, including me, fully understands. Sometimes, it's just too hard to fight the whole universe and be strong enough to come out ahead."

I gather Mariam up and envelop her in a hug as I whisper in her ear, "Promise me you'll keep trying. I'll be right by your side."

Mariam pulls away. "You'll pardon me if I'm a little skeptical. I've heard those kinds of promises before."

"You don't have to believe me in order for me to stay," I whisper.

Chapter Twelve

Mariam

"What's wrong with you, sweetheart?" my mom asks. "You barely touched your *kugel*."

As I take a bite of the savory potato casserole dish — a traditional Jewish recipe passed down through generations of my family, I attempt a smile. "It's delicious, Mom. I'm distracted by something at work."

My dad frowns. "Your job isn't too much for you, is it? Are you having a flare?"

"No, Dad, William and Isadora take great care of me."

My dad studies me carefully. "You need to eat then. Your mother worked hard on this meal. You look tired and pale."

Mindy gets up and stands behind my chair. She gently squeezes my shoulder before addressing my parents. "I know you guys are trying to help but it's merely adding to her stress."

My mom blinks in surprise. "I'm sorry, honey. We're just worried about you. You don't seem happy in your new job."

"Oh, I love working for Hallway Innovations. It's the best job I've ever had."

Elijah looks at me skeptically. "Jigger, jig, jig, then why do you look like you're about to cry?"

"It's complicated. I don't even know if I can explain it. I'm not even sure if I should."

Mindy studies me for a few moments and then blanches a ghostly shade of white. She looks up at my brother with tears in her eyes. "You know I've always used my gifts under strict rules, but your sister is my family now. I've gotta make an exception—"

"Mouse, jigger, jig, jig, I believe in you," Elijah answers. "You have your gift for a reason."

Mindy's struggle sends a chill up my spine. She has a history with our family. My sister-in-law's psychic gift has saved us from flying bullets. Her indecision has me holding my breath.

"Mariam, I know you want to protect William, but you need to tell him the truth," Mindy advises in a burst of speech.

Her words hit me like a punch in the gut. I don't even want to know how she knows. In a way, I'm glad not to be the only keeper of the secret. "You know this will kill him, right? He's told me those guys have been with him since the very beginning and he takes their word like the gospel truth."

Mindy nods. "I know. That's why you have to be the one to break the news to him. He trusts you more than anyone else right now."

"But if I tell him, he'll hate me. I couldn't bear

that."

"I can't imagine anyone hating my little girl," my dad interjects. "I guess you better explain. I don't want to be mad at your young man before I have a chance to formally meet him."

"I don't know how much I can say without Will's permission — which he can't give because he has no clue what's going on. But remember how conflicted you were before you tried to blow the whistle?"

"Please don't tell me this is going to turn out like that!" my mom exclaims. "Your father almost died for his convictions."

"I don't think it will be anything like Dad's situation. The only person likely to get hurt is William. I hate to see that happen because … well … I like him … a lot."

"Jigger, jig, jig, you might want to let Will know that too," Elijah suggests.

"When should I spill my little secret? After I tell him the devastating news? He may not be all that interested in my school-girl crush on him," I point out glumly.

"Jigger, jig, jig, I've only talked to him a few times, but I know him well enough to know even if his whole world was imploding around him, jigger, jig, jig, he'd be interested in knowing how you felt about him."

"Really? This isn't some prank you're pulling on me for kicks and giggles? I'm serious. I really like him, Elijah. I don't want to mess this up."

Mindy hugs me from behind. "Trust me, behind all his flash and good looks, there's a secretly shy guy who isn't so sure you like him either. You should tell him."

I look up at Mindy. "If your gift can tell this not-so-secretly-shy woman where to find her courage to have this conversation, it would be helpful."

"I don't have to tell you that. You've always had the strength. William needs your help. Go show him he has friends he can totally count on."

"Darn it! I hate it when you're right!" I tease.

"That's not the first time you've said that."

"I'm aware, but that doesn't make it any less true."

"You should take some leftovers with you. These conversations always go better with food," my mom offers.

My brother chuckles. "As good as my wife's intuition is, jigger, jig, jig, I wouldn't ignore Mom's advice."

<hr>

With a tight knot in my stomach, I pull up the accounting reports and put them on the large screen. Usually, I work in the front area with Isadora so I can provide backup on the phones and keep her company. She seems to feel more comfortable that way. But today, I need the privacy of my office.

Will sticks his head in the doorway and grins when he sees the plate of pastries. "What's the occasion?"

"My mom made homemade *gulch*. It's like a Jewish Danish with apricot jam and nuts."

Will grabs one and takes a bite. "This is a thousand times better than the protein bar in my backpack." He pauses to scrutinize me from head to toe. "You're all businesslike today. I love this look on you. Is there something on the schedule I forgot?"

"I guess you could say that. I need to talk to you about some discrepancies in the records."

Will's shoulders slump. "This doesn't sound good."

"Well, it's not all bad news. You're still insanely rich. You weren't wrong about that."

"That's a relief. I'm amazed you located enough records to find a discrepancy. I'm a bit of a slob, I don't know if you've noticed."

I choke back a nervous laugh. "The process wasn't easy. It took us months to locate everything and scan it in. I checked everything and verified it myself."

"Take a deep breath. I know you work hard. Whatever it is, just lay it on me."

"Maybe this is a good time for me to remind you that you hired me to be honest with you."

"I did. As I recall, you told me you had a tendency to be completely blunt and straightforward even in awkward situations."

I tuck my hair behind my ear. "I do. Which makes this supremely hard because I've come to really care for you as a friend. Well, if I'm honest, I like you a lot more than just a friend — and I'm afraid you'll hate me after this conversation."

"I can't promise I won't sulk a little, because that's what I do, but I promise I won't hate you."

My lips turn up in a ghost of a smile. "That's okay. I'm used to sulking. I have a little brother, remember?"

"Ha, ha, you're so funny I forgot to laugh."

I raise an eyebrow. "Like I've never heard that one

before —"

Will pulls up a chair and looks at my computer screen. "You better break the news before I lose my nerve and go out for coffee."

I draw in a deep breath and let it out. "Okay, as you know we've been reconstructing your banking records. Some of them we could get electronically, others we had to hand type from the paper copies we retrieved from your so-called archiving system. Your accountant gave us some tax information as well."

"So, if I ever run for political office, I'm covered, right?"

"I'm not sure I'd go that far, but you're in much better shape than before I started. Anyway, I haven't looked into the Hallway Innovations side of things yet. Right now, all we're talking about is the Heart Wish Foundation—"

He swallows hard. "Maybe I should've gone for coffee."

"Think of this like ripping off a Band-Aid. We need to get it over with. Now we have systems in place so it won't happen again."

"So what won't happen again? The suspense is killing me!"

"I'm getting there. Based on the information we reconstructed, we built case files for each family the Heart Wish Foundation assisted. HWF claimed expenses for thirty-seven charitable causes or families."

Will's chest puffs up a little as he grins. "Yeah, we've done a lot of good work in a short amount of time."

"You have. Please don't let what I'm about to tell

you diminish the pride you're feeling right now. I've read the thank-you letters of the families you've helped. You changed their whole world."

"I guess you better tell me the bad news."

"Like I said, we built case files for each child or family HWF has helped. We collected receipts, canceled checks, photographs, news reports, emails, letters, thank you notes and anything else we could find."

"I take it some 'children' came up missing?" he asks with an expression of dread.

As much as I'm trying to hide it, my eyes are brimming with tears. "I'm so sorry. I looked for three weeks for other explanations. I even brought in Identity Bank to see if they could help me. I am pretty good with spreadsheets because I had to compile data as part of my graduate work, but I didn't make a mistake."

"So, how did you figure it out?"

"It was like you guessed. There were three cases that were taken as charitable deductions on the foundation's taxes that we couldn't find any matching receipts for. Yet the amounts withdrawn were always the same."

"How much was I taken for?"

"Slightly less than one hundred and fifty thousand dollars," I answer with a grimace.

"Oh, is that all? I thought you were talking about big money —"

"That is big money! It would buy a house. Okay, maybe not a very luxurious house — but still a house!"

"Point taken. Okay, so … who is the slimy jerk who stole money from a charity? Even worse, who took money from me? I didn't let very many people on the inside."

"I hope you don't mind, but I had Isaac and Tristan look into it because I knew you would have questions."

"Are you kidding? Isaac with his connections? Identity Bank would've been my first call anyway. I hope Isaac and his former colleagues at the FBI, and whatever clandestine agency he used to work for, have this pissant in their sights."

"I don't actually know. I heard they were trying to find a guy named Steve Banfield."

"Steve? Stevo screwed me? *No freakin' way!* He was always telling me how much he believed in the dream and how underdogs like us had to stick together. I've known him since high school. I would have bet my life he had my back."

"I'm so sorry. I hate this for you."

"Do you know how they figured it out?"

"Tristan said they were able to do some handwriting analysis and caught him on a surveillance camera cashing one of the checks."

"I guess I should've known something was up. He was always so jealous of the cars. Every time I spent a dime of my own money on myself he would be beside himself with rage. I should've taken that as a sign. I just chalked it up to car envy."

"You couldn't have known it would lead to this."

"Oh man! He's known me for years and he has access to everything. How do I know he's only stolen a hundred and fifty thousand?"

"I guess you don't for sure. Madison's husband

Trevor used to be a forensic accountant. Maybe he knows somebody who can help us. In the meantime, I think you need to talk to your future brother-in-law about locking down all online accounts. Jameson is pretty good at all that stuff."

"Are you kidding me? If I wanted him to, Jameson could create a whole new identity for me and I could completely disappear."

"You saying that's what you want to do?" I ask.

"Nah, I'm having too much fun proving everybody wrong right here with you. Besides, I want to be front and center when this pipsqueak has to face justice."

As upsetting as this day has been, I take an unseemly amount of pride in the fact that William doesn't want to chuck it all and take a never-ending vacation to someplace warm and tropical. For today, that will have to be enough of a win. At least he doesn't hate me.

CHAPTER THIRTEEN

WILL

THE HEAVY BAG SWINGS back and almost knocks me to the ground when I fail to duck quickly enough. I punch it again. How could I be so stupid? I naively trusted my friends to have the same vision for Hallway Innovations as me. I thought everyone had my back.

Obviously not. Stevo — and who knows how many other people — had the balls to lie right to my face. I should've listened to Kendall. She is always telling me to be more careful, but I keep blowing her off and telling her she is paranoid. It turns out she was right to be worried. Now I have to figure out how to fix it. Unfortunately, I'm way better at fixing technical problems than I am at fixing relationships between people.

I let loose with another flurry of punches as I try to work through my rage with myself and the person I thought was my friend. The sound of rhythmic punching is broken by the shrill ring of my cell phone.

Sitting down on an old bar stool in the basement, I answer the phone without even looking at it. "Help, I need you!" Mariam's voice is so weak, I pull the phone away from my ear to confirm it's her number.

"Do I need to call an ambulance?"

"No, please don't. Just come help me," she pleads in a hoarse whisper.

"Hang on! I'll be there as soon as I can." If I thought my heart was racing from pounding on my heavy bag, it was nothing compared to how it feels now as I throw on some sweats. I wonder if I should call Elijah. But if she wanted her brother there, she would've called him herself.

I know I'm exceeding every speed limit in existence on the way over to Mariam's place. I couldn't care less if I get pulled over. In fact, it might work in my favor since I don't exactly know what's wrong. Having a police escort might not be such a bad idea. I'm desperately trying to remember everything Mariam has ever told me about her fibro. I know she hurts every single day, but I don't remember her ever telling me it was a life-threatening disease.

After I pull into her driveway, I slam the car into park and run up to the door. Of course, it's locked! I sprint toward the garage and lift the awkward metal door. I breathe a sigh of relief when the door to her kitchen opens without any resistance.

Her townhouse is eerily quiet and dark. I turn on the flashlight on my phone and search for Mariam. I don't find her in a cursory search of the kitchen and living room area downstairs, so I quickly go upstairs. As soon as I hit the top landing of the stairs, I hear Mariam breathing heavily and whimpering in pain. I make my way toward the sound and find a light switch along the way. When I get to Mariam's bedroom, I see her sprawled on the hardwood floor wearing only a tiny tank top and shorts. She is trembling so violently I can see her body shaking from the doorway. Tears are running down her face.

I rush to her side and kneel down. "What happened, Mar?"

She appears to have trouble focusing her eyes. "GQ?"

I look down at my sweaty T-shirt with the arms torn off and paint-stained sweatpants. "I'm not so GQ today, but yeah it's me, Will. What are you doing on the floor?"

Mariam's brows furrow. "I … I don't know."

"I don't suppose the why matters so much right now. Let's get you into bed. You're like an icicle."

"Don't touch me! I hurt!" Mariam protests.

"Are you feeling strong enough to stand on your own?" I ask as I study the situation.

More tears squeeze from the corners of her eyes. "Don't think so, I'm still on the floor."

"How long have you been there, babe?" I whisper, trying to keep my voice even.

"Probably hours," she admits as a new round of shivers overtakes her body.

I stand up and walk over to her linen closet. I remove a large comforter and another blanket. Fighting back tears, I cover her with the blanket and then unfurl the comforter and lay it on the floor next to her. "Mariam, I'm so sorry. I'm going to touch you and it'll probably hurt, but I'll try to limit the damage, I swear."

"What are you planning to do?" she asks, her speech slurred and barely audible.

"I'm going to slide this fluffy comforter under you to help cushion you as I lift you. Unfortunately, I'll have to jostle you a little to get it in position."

"It's okay. You're a nice guy—" Mariam's voice falls off as if she has no more strength.

Carefully, I inch the blanket under her, cringing every time I have to roll her. It seems that the slightest touch causes her to cry out in pain. After the blanket is completely under her body, I pull the corners up around her shoulders and help her to a sitting position.

Once she is sitting, she rouses a bit and looks around. "Mariam, do you think you hit your head?"

She tries to shake her head. "No, already had a headache. So dizzy. Stupid fibro. Guess I didn't make it to bed."

"Almost there. I'm going to lift you up now." As gracefully as I can, I lift Mariam and place her on the bed. She groans when her body touches the pillows and the mattress. Honestly, I can't tell if it's from pain or from sheer relief of not being on the hardwood floor anymore. I tuck in the surrounding blankets.

"Thank you," she mumbles.

"Is there anything else you need? Are you hungry or anything?"

"I need some pain medicine and my muscle relaxers. They're on the kitchen table."

"Okay, hang tight. Be right back."

In her kitchen, I easily find her medication. Everything in her kitchen is neat and orderly. I'm not sure why I expected anything different. As I pick up the bottle, I notice a warning which suggests the medication should be taken with food. I'm not a gourmet chef. To be honest, I eat most of my meals out. It's the curse of being a single guy. Maybe there will be something in her fridge. I breathe a sigh of relief when I see leftover soup from her favorite deli. I know she took it home from lunch a couple days ago. I think I can manage to warm it up with some toast.

As I take the hastily prepared meal upstairs, I'm thrilled to see Mariam is resting comfortably and no longer shivering. When I set the tray down next to the bed, she opens her eyes wide. "What are you doing?"

"Bringing you your medication and a little something to eat," I explain, puzzled by her reaction.

Mariam reaches up and holds her head for a second. "Sorry, I knew that. Just had a second of fibro fog."

"'Fibro fog'? You haven't mentioned that in a while."

"Sometimes, my brain is all jumbled. Like today."

"Another day, when things are clearer, you can explain. In the meantime, you should have some dinner and take your pain medication so you feel better. Let me help you sit up."

"Oh, I got it. Elijah used to write books in bed, so this is an adjustable bed."

Mariam pushes a button on a remote and puts the head and feet of the bed up.

"Nice! Those will be on the list when I get a place."

I set the tray over Mariam's lap. "Do you need anything else?"

"You're not leaving, are you?" Mariam asks.

"Not until you tell me to. I was planning to go downstairs and let you eat in peace."

"I don't want you to go." Mariam pats the large queen-size bed. "Stay here and keep me company. I'm tired of being alone."

Dozens of thoughts spin in my brain and only a few are actually helpful. I take a deep breath and remind myself Mariam is sick and not feeling up to dealing with the direction the rest of my thoughts are going.

"Uh… when you called, I was in the middle of a workout. You probably don't want to be that close to me right now."

"So? Take a shower," Mariam answers as she takes a bite of soup.

I chuckle. "We may be really good friends and all, but you're still teeny. I don't think we could share clothes like BFFs."

Mariam nibbles on a piece of toast. "Silly man. My brother left a bunch of clothes in the spare room. If you don't mind Adrian O'Brien concert T-shirts, you should be good."

— • —

Waking up like this is something I could definitely get used to. Mariam's arm is draped over my stomach and her cheek is resting on my chest. Her hair is billowed out in a soft fragrant cloud across her face. Her breathing has slowed, and she finally looks at peace.

Mariam works so hard to hide her pain from me — and everyone else, I rarely get a glimpse of how much it impacts her. I know she gets terrible headaches and fights fatigue and pain every day, but most days she would rather get dental work done without Novocain than let me know anything is bothering her.

I suspect things had to be dire for her to let me see her in this state. Even though it scares the crap out of me, I'm glad she did. It helps me understand what she's dealing with. It means the world to me that she trusts me enough to let me into her world of pain.

Mariam sighs, reminding me that this gift of closeness won't last forever. I concentrate on matching my breathing pattern to hers and soon drift back to sleep.

The next time I wake up, Mariam is shaking again. I resist the urge to bolt out of bed for fear I might hurt her, but I wonder if I accidentally kicked her or something.

I take a deep breath and blow it out my nose before I greet, "Good morning, Gorgeous. How are you feeling?"

Mariam extracts herself from my chest and gingerly moves over to her side of the bed as tears roll down her face. "I was hoping all this was just a terrible nightmare, but it's not. I am so stiff this morning, I can barely move. I'm in a full-blown flare — the worst I've had in ages."

I reach over and brush her hair out of her eyes. "I hate that fibromyalgia is such a nightmare for you. I would do anything to fix that for you. But I have to be honest, being here, spending time with you and helping you, is anything but a nightmare for me. It's kinda like a dream come true."

Mariam grabs a Kleenex off her nightstand and wipes away her tears. "Okay, you're right. You do have unexpected knight-in-shining-armor tendencies. If my body wasn't burning with pain, this would be downright dreamy."

"Given the circumstances, I'll take that as a compliment."

CHAPTER FOURTEEN

MARIAM

"OH, COME ON, IT'LL be fun!" I tease with a snort of laughter. "Isn't that what you told me?" I have to hold on tight as Will maneuvers his nimble sports car around a tight corner.

When we slow down for traffic, Will scowls at me. "Yeah, it was fun when you were the one trying on clothes. I have freakishly long arms. Nothing ever fits me. That's why I only have two suits."

"Is that why you always roll up your sleeves? I thought you were trying to be like some walking, talking sex symbol."

The tips of Will's ears turn red as he shrugs. "There might have been some swagger going on, but mostly my shirts usually hit me about mid-forearm. If I buy them at the big and tall store, they look like one of Kendall's dresses."

"Huh, you know that's how Cristiano and Jordan met, right? He couldn't find any clothes that fit, either. Tell her what bugs you, it's kinda what she does for a living."

"We always shopped at thrift stores or got hand-me-downs from the church when I was growing up. Even though I can get custom clothes now, it never occurs to me."

I raise an eyebrow. "Help me understand. You buy all these insanely expensive cars, but you don't do small things to take care of yourself. Why?"

"Well, I explained part of it — you know contracts, leases and all that. I'm working on it. It helps that you and Izzy have helped me get my business in order. I talked to Jeff about my learning issues and the way I process things. He told me he would be happy to review any legal documents for me and break them down into steps I can understand. I don't know if I'll take him up on it, but just knowing he has my back is a huge relief."

"And the other part?"

Will sits tall against the rich leather in his convertible. He reaches out for my hand. "Ah … the cars. Cars were my one positive connection with my dad. Norman Kordes was the ultimate gear head. He loved cars. Old cars, new cars, big cars, little cars, pickups, convertibles, station wagons or jeeps, it didn't matter … my dad loved them all. More importantly, they made him happy. When he was working on a new project car, he would cut back on his drinking and all of his attention would be focused on restoring the car. We would study magazines together and plan out paint schemes and pick parts from junkyards and rummage sales."

For a few moments, Will concentrates on driving through some traffic but then resumes his train of thought. "Yeah, my dad and I were buddies then. One time, he couldn't find a part he needed to rebuild an engine, and I fabricated one for him. It was the only time I ever remember him being proud of me."

"I'm sorry. You deserved more."

"We did deserve more, but honestly, I don't know if my dad could have given more. I'm not sure he was capable of it. So, I collect cars to remind myself of the good times we had together and to drown out the sound of my dad's voice in my head."

Will's expression is filled with pain. I lay my hand on his thigh.

Will pounds the steering wheel. "He had no right to say that to his own son! I am not a retarded loser. I have a job and if I had a family, I could support them. He sure as heck didn't support his family. I know — because it became my job the day he left."

"You're right. No parent — or anyone else — should ever say those words. You are not a loser. He was wrong. The people who matter know that."

"Part of me wishes Tristan would just find his deadbeat butt so he would finally know too. As much as I hate him, there's a part of me that still loves him. Even so, I'd like to see him have to eat his words and apologize to my mother and Kendall. He put us through way too much."

"Would an apology make all that much difference after all these years?"

"I suppose it would matter if he means it. The man would be a stranger to me now. He probably wouldn't even recognize me."

After we pull up in front of Jordan's studio, Will

comes around the car to help me get out of the low-slung sports car. When I stand up, I throw my arms around his neck and kiss him.

"I don't recognize the guy your dad described either. The William Benjamin Kordes I know is brilliantly funny, scary bright and compassionate beyond all imagination. He is creative, helpful and stands up to bullies. He helps countless people without taking any of the glory. That's the kind of man I want in my life. I don't know what kind of measuring stick your dad was using, but it was clearly faulty. Your dad either didn't know you very well or wasn't paying attention."

"Is that really how you see me or are you just trying to make me feel better?" Will asks as he braces himself against his car. His face is tight with tension.

I draw my hand down his cheek. "Remember, I promised I would always tell you the truth even when it's hard for you to hear? You have exceeded my expectations in more ways than I ever thought possible."

Will smiles down at me. "When we first met, you told me people didn't like your tendency to tell it like it is. Personally, I kinda dig it. You have a knack for telling me things I didn't even know I needed to hear."

The heat in Will's eyes is intense. I've seen this sort of thing happen to other people, but it's never occurred to me. I hold statue-still in anticipation.

Will threads his fingers through my hair, leans down and places his lips next to mine. "I don't want to hurt you, but I've been dying to do this forever. Please tell me if it hurts."

I close my eyes and revel in the crush of his lips on

mine. I couldn't tell you if there's pain involved because all I'm feeling is a sense that all is right in my world. How can a guy who seems so wrong on so many levels make me feel this way?

⸻ ◆ ⸻

"Oh, shoot! You have another headache, don't you?" Isadora asks as she rushes into my office carrying cups of steaming hot coffee in a drink holder. After she carefully sets it down on my desk, she frantically looks around the office. "Crap! This won't make it any better. Where's Mr. K?"

I turn up the desk lamp a bit more to illuminate my nearly pitch-black work-area. "He's in his office. Why? What's wrong?" I ask as I take in her nervous energy and pensive expression.

Izzy picks up the drinks and heads toward Will's office. "That's probably better anyway. He has a flat screen TV in his office."

When we enter, Will has his back turned, and he's sketching on his iPad. He has his headphones in, so at first, he doesn't even hear us. But, it doesn't take him long to smell the coffee. He quickly turns and takes the headphones out of his ears and greets us with a smile. "Oh, let me guess … you're here to show Izzy all those pictures you took of me at Jordan's the other day, aren't you? Just a second, I'll pull them up on the iPad. But … if I have to show her pictures of me in the funny little muslin suit, you have to show pictures of your gorgeous red dress. It's only fair." Will shoots me a wide grin and winks. He turns to Izzy. "I know I should wait until my sister's wedding to show you, but I can't. Mariam is too much of a knockout to keep under wraps."

"I'd like to see those pictures sometime, Mr. K. — but not today," she answers somberly. The tone in her voice makes my stomach drop.

"What's up, Izzy?"

Izzy walks over to his television and picks up his remote. "Do you still record the morning shows every day?"

Will nods. "Sometimes I find worthy causes that way."

Izzy picks a show and cues it to a local news segment. "I'm so sorry, Mr. K. I heard this playing when I went to go get coffee." She cringes as she presses play.

I reach out to hold Will's hand as we listen to a studious newscaster announce, "Unsettling news regarding local philanthropist, Will Kordes. A family has come forward leveling some serious charges against his charity alleging the whole thing is a sham which discriminates against sick, defenseless children. We've reached out to Mr. Kordes, but we have yet to receive a statement. Join us tonight at eleven when we explore the tragedy that has befallen the Heywood family. We will hear how our local hero has failed to come to their rescue. We plan to talk to Mrs. Heywood and her attorney and find out exactly how they intend to proceed against Mr. Kordes."

The female anchor turns to her coworker. "Wow! I met Will Kordes. He seemed so passionate about his work. If it's all a sham, he had me fooled. I look forward to the story tonight and I'm sure all of you do too. Now, we need to turn it over to Levi for some late-breaking traffic news."

I let go of Will's hand and cover my mouth in

horror. I'd like to say I'm totally shocked by what I just heard, but given what the Heywoods have already pulled, this little stunt wasn't completely out of the realm of possibility. Like Izzy said, the woman always was "cray-cray".

Izzy turns off the television and picks up her cup of coffee. She is waiting anxiously for Will to respond.

My head is pounding so hard I'm dizzy and nauseous. It's becoming progressively more difficult to follow the action.

Will twirls a pen between his fingers as he tries to look casual — yet I can tell he's feeling anything but. His jaw is clenched and his blue eyes are cold as ice. He picks his phone up off his desk and hands it over to me. "You better take this. If you don't, I'm likely to make a few choice phone calls that any lawyer in his or her right mind would advise me not to make — you know like to the news media or to a deranged mother and her son who likes to fake his disability."

Izzy's eyes widen. "So, what are we going to do? Do we just let them tell a bunch of lies about us? I read every piece of information about all the people you've helped. I know you are one hundred percent legit. I knew she was shady, but I didn't think she was this lame."

I choke on the coffee I was sipping. "Izzy! Why don't you tell us how you really feel?" I respond, unable to control my laughter.

"What? It's true! We've already caught them in a lie and they think they'll court and challenge us. I only have a GED, but even I know when you go to court you have to swear to tell the truth and nothing but the truth."

I lean against Will's desk. "Isadora is right, you know. We don't have to do anything. Their case will fall apart on its own."

"But, won't I look stupid if I don't fight back?"

I shake my head and immediately regret the movement. I wince in pain.

"Are you okay?" Will asks as he gets up from his chair and motions for me to sit down.

"I'm fine, I just have a bad headache. I'm on the verge of a flare."

"Have you taken your meds?"

"Yeah, I took them a few minutes ago. I was hoping the caffeine in the coffee would help stave it off. Anyway, you can't play in the dirt with Shayna Heywood. If you do, you'll only end up covered in mud."

"So, what am I supposed to do, just take it?"

"I didn't say that. You have to be the grown-up in the room."

Will smirks. "You remember who you're talking to, right?"

"I do, that's why I know you can do this."

"You have more faith in me than I do," Will admits.

"That's okay. You've got Izzy and me to back you up."

"I'm supposed to back him up? I don't know what to do!" Izzy exclaims.

"Iz, you may be a teenager, but you are one of the smartest, most levelheaded people I know. After all, you outwitted a deranged kidnapper for months and kept his children safe. Not many adults I know could accomplish that. I trust you to handle anything that comes up at Heart Wish Foundation. Pushy reporters or mouthy mothers barely make you bat an eyelash."

Isadora blushes. "Okay, I see what you mean. You're right. Bring 'em on."

Will puts his hands up in a timeout gesture. "Not so fast. We don't even know what we're planning to say."

I log into Will's computer and pull up a file. I read it aloud to the group. "The Heart Wish Foundation is incredibly proud of the work we have done nationwide. The individuals and families we serve come to us in their most vulnerable times and everything they share with HWF is confidential. Every applicant's circumstances are evaluated with great care and diligence. We try our best to meet each applicant's actual needs while making the experience as joyful as possible. We regret that we cannot serve every applicant, but we do not discriminate based on age, race, national origin, disability or sexual orientation. To respect the privacy of our applicants, there will be no further comment."

"Oh, man!" Will replies. "Mariam, you totally undersold your skills. You should've been in PR! That's perfect."

"It is the bomb! When did you come up with that?" Izzy asks.

I shrug. "To be honest, I drafted something the same day you started working on your denial letter. I had a hunch we hadn't seen the last of the Heywoods."

Completely disregarding Izzy, Will catches my face between his hands and brushes a light kiss across my lips. "That's why I hire the absolute best."

I blush bright red. "Just trying to think ahead."

"Izzy, will you please put a press release out to the local news stations and papers? If you don't know how to do that, call Madison. She can help you. She used to work at a newspaper. I'm going to take Mariam and get out of the office before I am tempted to do something I shouldn't. I need to forget all about Hallway Innovations and the Heart Wish Foundation for a few hours."

"Okay, I can make that statement or say no comment if they press further. If I've learned anything over the past few years, it's how to tell reporters to take a flying leap."

Will walks over and gives her a high five. "Iz? Have I told you today how awesome you are?"

"Nope, not today," she answers with a shy grin.

"Well, consider yourself told."

"M'kay, thanks."

"Okay, I'll see you later, I'm running away from my job for a while, like the grown-up I am," Will teases.

"I don't blame you. It sounds like the best plan ever. Have fun."

CHAPTER FIFTEEN

WILL

I LOOK UP AT the massive rock wall in total awe. "This place is epic. What are we doing here?"

Mariam smiles. "You said you needed to get away from your life. Aidan's rock wall is about as far from reality as you can get. I took the liberty of calling an impromptu meeting of the Girlfriend Posse."

I glance around at the large group of people congregating in Aidan O'Brien's large workout room with floor-to-ceiling rock formations. "Um … I hate to break it to you, but this isn't just a few girlfriends meeting for lunch. The whole gang is here. I think everyone who was at Phoenix and Zoe's wedding is here — plus a few extras."

Madison slides down the last few feet of her rope and joins our conversation. "The Girlfriend Posse has grown over the years. Technically, our group is still composed of only women. However, almost every time we meet, we drag the guys along."

A burst of laughter bubbles up. "Girlfriend Posse?

You guys don't seem particularly dangerous—"

Tara turns around with a sage expression. "You haven't had the pleasure of seeing this group handle a crisis. It is something to behold." Tara places her arm around Mariam's shoulders. "I saw the newscast this morning. I take it that's why you called an emergency meeting of the Girlfriend Posse?"

Mariam turns pale and rubs her temple. "I don't know if it will help, but I didn't know what else to do."

"Do? I thought we weren't doing anything," I reply as my frustration with the whole situation comes roaring back.

Mariam pats my forearm in a placating manner. "At the moment … we're not. You go play crazy adventurer with my brother and his friends. My friends and I are going to go vent about all the undesirables on the planet and what we would do if we were in charge of the world. Go burn off some of your anger and frustration. That's what we're here for; besides, Aidan's wall of wonder is incredibly fun. If my muscles weren't completely fried from my flare, I would be climbing right beside you matching you hold for hold."

"Are you sure you'll be okay?" I ask as I watch her sway a little.

"Yeah, it's been a long day. I'm going to gorge myself on Heather's cookies and sweet tea. I'll catch you later." Mariam stands on her tiptoes and brushes a kiss across my lips.

Well then! I guess we're taking our relationship public. This is news to me. Welcome news, but news nonetheless.

Like a puppy watching his kid go to school, I watch her leave the room. For several moments, I silently stand

and stare at the doorway where she just stood. Elijah comes over and claps me on the shoulder. "Jigger, jig, jig, never thought I'd see the day—"

Elijah's words shake me out of my love stupor. "Huh?"

He chuckles. "Jigger, jig, jig, I was just saying, you did the impossible. You got my big sis to change her mind. Jigger, jig, jig, I don't know if I've ever seen that happen before. Congratulations!"

Jeff nods. "Mariam can be a prickly one. You seem to have figured out how to get past her defenses. That's not always easy."

"The way things are going right now, Mariam may be sorry she ever met me. I don't know if you've heard, but there are people out there who are trying to destroy everything I've built."

"*¡Idiota!*" Jude mutters in Spanish. "I will never understand what makes people do things like that."

Aidan unclips his climbing harness and shakes his head. "Oh yeah, Jude and Tasha know all about idiots. Jude's mother-in-law is one of the biggest idiots on the planet. Talk about a psychologically unbalanced woman with an ax to grind. Jude can give you a few lessons on how to deal with that crazy mother."

I glance over at the unassuming musician with the odd colored eyes. I haven't had a chance to talk to him much. Although I've seen him in concert a couple times. "Yeah? I need all the help I can get."

Jude meets my gaze with a strange intensity. "I hope you mean it. The only way you can win over a bully like her is with the help of your friends. At first, Tasha tried to ignore her mom's destructive comments and behaviors. But soon, they became too much. We had to come up with a plan to help take her down."

I rub my hands together with glee. "I like the sound of that. This sitting back and doing nothing doesn't sit well with me. I am a doer. I like to fix things that are wrong."

Aidan walks over and lays a hand on my shoulder. "I wish Logan was here. If he was, he would tell you that you can't take this on directly."

"Logan?" I ask, trying to follow the conversation.

"Logan is my security guy. He's ex-military and one of the smartest strategists I've ever known. He'd tell you to stay out of the line of fire and let your team take the heat."

The corner of my lip curls up. "I don't know if you've noticed, but I don't have much of a team. The closest thing I've got is my twin, Kendall. She's pretty tough, but she's in the middle of getting ready to get married. I'm not willing to put her in the line of fire."

Aidan guffaws with a loud burst of laughter. "With all due respect, your sister puts herself exactly where she wants to be. I know her well enough to know that she would take bullets for you. I also know there's a long list of people in this town who are on your team, my daughter included. Do you think every call out of the Girlfriend Posse gets this kind of turnout?"

"Maybe?" I answer tentatively.

Jude shakes his head. "Negative. I've been around a long time. This is unusual, especially for a relative newcomer."

Rocco nods. "Even Mallory and I are in on this

one. She figured she could do something through *Word Soup PNW*. You have the full contingent today."

"Then why? You guys barely know me."

"That's not true. We've seen what you've done for Maddie, Locate My Heart and a dozen other people in our community. You could have done it to get famous or to get women, but you didn't. You went out of your way to help families and programs simply because it was the right thing to do. That tells me everything I need to know."

"What if other people believe Shayna Heywood's lies? She could ruin the Heart Wish Foundation."

"Like I said, she's an *idiota*. She only thinks she has all the power," Jude insists. "People who bluster like that collapse when confronted with the truth."

"That's what I said! But, Mariam said it would be a waste of my time to challenge her credibility."

Jeff nods. "I agree with your girlfriend. You are the public face of your business. You need to keep your hands clean. Let us help you."

"How can you guys help me? This woman is not telling the truth."

Aidan grins. "She has no idea what she's up against. Mariam had the foresight to call a meeting of the Girlfriend Posse."

Confused, I look around the room at the knowing grins. "I guess I'm lost. I don't understand."

"You will. The Girlfriend Posse is known for pulling off the impossible. I don't expect your case to be any different."

Rocco slaps me on the back. "Unfortunately, I have

to go to work, but Mallory and her friends are a sight to behold. You might want to buckle up it could be a wild ride."

Balancing carefully on the top of the wall, I throw my fist in the air. "Is Mariam a genius, or what? She told me rock climbing would be the answer to all of my problems and she was totally on point!"

Jude joins me at the top of the wall. "*Amigo*, you say that only because you made it to the top first this time," he teases.

"It only took me three times to beat you to the top. I just got lucky. Seriously, thank you for the competition — and the pointers. You made this fun."

"*No problemo*. That's what friends are —" We are interrupted when the door opens and Aidan's wife sticks her head in the door.

The usually unflappable Tara looks distressed as she yells up to me. "Sorry to bother you, but Mariam needs your help."

"She asked for me?" I blurt in surprise. "That's unusual."

"Well, not exactly. She didn't want to bother anybody, but she still needs help. I wish Rocco was still here."

I throw my leg over the wall and rappel down. I spew more than a few cuss words when my rope gets caught around my leg and slows me down.

Tara smiles at me gently. "Relax, a few seconds won't make a huge difference. I'm sure Mariam would rather have you there in one piece."

When I free myself from the rope and the harness, I ask, "What's wrong?"

Tara gives me a quick hug and puts her arm around my waist as we walk out of the workout room. "It's been a really tough day, and I'm sure it's all catching up with her."

"Why didn't she say anything? I've just been playing around all afternoon to try to get my mind off of the dumpster fire that's going on at the Heart Wish Foundation right now."

"I have my theory, but it would only be a guess. You'll have to talk to Mariam when she's feeling better."

"I heard you were psychic or something like that. Shouldn't you have the answers to all of this?"

Tara chuckles softly as she shakes her head. "I wish it worked that way, but I don't control my visions. Besides, even if I did, I can only share if it's a matter of life and death."

"I suppose it's a no news is good news kinda deal, huh?"

"In this case, I think so. The fact that Mariam trusts you to help her is a very good thing."

Tara leads me into her living room. Mariam is lying on a large couch. Her feet are propped up on pillows and Tasha is taking her blood pressure. Maddie is sitting beside her on the couch holding an ice pack on her head. When I approach, Maddie puts a finger up to her lips, cautioning me to be quiet.

I lean down and kiss Mariam's cheek gently. "What's up?"

"GQ?" she mumbles without opening her eyes.

"Yeah, but thanks to you today I am a stellar alpinist."

Her face contorts with pain. "Cute wordplay. My head is going to explode and my whole right side is on fire. I want to go home."

"Mar! Why didn't you say something? We could've left hours ago."

"You have enough problems in your life today. I didn't want to be one more."

"Don't be silly, you could never —"

Abruptly, she leans over and throws up in a dishpan. Maddie pulls the ice pack away from her head and exclaims, "Oh no, there she goes again. Her poor tummy! I hope her mom makes her chicken soup like my mom does when I'm sick." She looks up at Tara. "Mom, can you make her some? Your soup is like magic."

Tara looks uncomfortable. "You know, Aunt Keira's or Aunt Heather's is much better than mine."

While this conversation is playing in the background, I glance over at Tasha. "This isn't the first time? She seems pretty bad. Should I make a stop at the hospital instead?"

Tasha gives me a tight nod. "I'm not a doctor. But as a nurse and her friend, I think she should go. Her pain is off the charts. They could give her something stronger than what she's got at home. Her vitals indicate she's dehydrated."

"I'm right here," Mariam argues from the couch. "Going to the hospital takes forever. I don't know if I have that many spoons left."

I squat down beside the couch. "Mariam, I would give you every spoon in the whole silverware drawer if I could. If I can make the hospital trip as painless as possible, will you go?"

Tears flow down her face. She nods. "So tired of hurting. Please make it stop."

"I'll do what I can."

I brush a light kiss across her cheek and wipe her tears away with my thumb before I hug Maddie briefly. "I need to borrow your mom for a minute. Do you have your cell phone?"

Maddie nods solemnly and points to the backpack on her wheelchair. I pull her cell phone out and hand it to her. "Can you unlock it for me?"

She quickly complies and hands it back. I program my cell phone number in her phone. "If you need me, I'll be in the next room trying to figure things out. Give me a call and I'll be right here, okay?"

"Are you going to be like my daddy?"

"What do you mean?"

"Before I met him, everything was awful and I hurt all the time. Then, I met him and my mom. They adopted me. Dad did some magic and now my life is perfect."

"Oh, I see."

"Miss Mariam needs a really big magic trick," Maddie replies wistfully.

"She certainly does. I don't think anyone has ever said a truer thing in my whole life. I'm so glad you believe in magic. I'm trying really hard to believe too."

CHAPTER SIXTEEN

MARIAM

THE CNA CLICKS HER tongue at me as she sees the iPad on my lap. "I thought you were supposed to be resting." She checks my blood pressure and nods her approval. "This is better than it was this morning. Try to get some sleep."

I jump when William sticks his head around the curtain. He's carrying a big bouquet of balloons and brightly colored tulips. "Morning, Sunshine! Feeling better today?" He sets the bouquet down and walks over to the bed. He leans down and thoroughly kisses me.

"Hmm, never mind — I can see you won't be getting much sleep. However, this guy should be a nice distraction from the icky stuff. I wouldn't mind if he treated my bumps and bruises," the CNA teases.

Will winks at me. "Sorry, these days, I only look after my favorite patient. How is she doing?"

"I'm trying to get her to lay off work for a while and get some rest. Do you think you can convince her?"

"Well, since technically I am her boss, I guess I

could order her to take a vacation."

The CNA smiles at him. "Please do, medicine can only do so much."

"All this lying around is driving me crazy," I protest.

"I understand." Will looks up at the clock on the wall "Hey, Madison has a diversion for you. She said to watch her show at nine thirty this morning. Do you have Internet here?"

I raise an eyebrow. "Yeah, I was working on expense reports for you. I guess that's not so great for my headache. But I was so bored, I had to do something."

"Did your doctor say when you get to go home?"

"My labs looked good this morning. My medication levels are almost balanced. He said we're shooting for discharge tomorrow."

"How is your pain?"

"Much better. I'm glad you convinced me to come. I think the new medicines are helping a lot."

Will perches on the edge of my bed and types Madison's website into the browser. I scoot over so he can sit next to me. When her site comes up, and he sees the graphic, his jaw drops open. "What in the heck? Did you know about this? Holy —"

"Relax, it's all part of the plan," I explain.

"What plan?"

"I told you — the Girlfriend Posse doesn't play."

"I thought Madison owns a horse farm where she breeds Arabian horses. Doesn't her show mainly deal with music stuff, like feel-good stories, news about pop stars, and other lighthearted topics?"

I shrug. "It does now because that's what she chooses to cover since the birth of her daughter. However, she used to be an investigative reporter in Boston. I have a hunch she'll be flexing those muscles today. Mallory is going to back her up with an article in *Word Soup*."

"Whoo-hoo!" Will cheers, but then covers his mouth when he remembers where he is. "Too bad her show is only a podcast. I wish she was on network news."

As Madison's podcast cuts to a commercial, I explain, "Funny you should mention that ... because of Madison's chops as a reporter, her stories are often picked up by various news stations and re-broadcast. I wouldn't be surprised if this goes viral. Who knows what kind of coverage Mallory's article will get since she won a prestigious journalism award for a case she covered recently?"

I am mouth the word "Wow!" as I train my eyes on Mallory's iPad. After the commercial, the show cuts back to a split screen between Shayna and Robert Heywood and Madison Black. "I want to thank you so much for coming forward to tell your story. I'd like to give you a moment to give us some background, and then I'll ask you some questions about things my viewers might want to know, does that sound fair?" Madison asks with a pleasant smile.

Shayna nods. "I gave you a copy of the application materials I submitted to the Heart Wish Foundation. It's ridiculous to have to provide all that private information. Honestly, I only gave it to you because Robert's diagnosis is so complicated I can't remember all the fancy medical names for his condition." She points to Robert sitting next to her in his wheelchair. He is slumped over with some drool on his chin. "As you can see, my son is extremely sick. He gets worse every day and he might not have very long to live, but does the Heart Wish Foundation care? No!"

"What makes you say that, Mrs. Heywood?"

"Are you retarded?" Shayna snaps back. "I'm saying that because the so-called charitable foundation turned us down cold. My son asked to go to a video game conference he's wanted to go to his whole life. It was a simple request, and they didn't care about my poor, dying son. So, I think the whole organization is one big scam. I don't think they've ever helped anyone. I'm here to expose them for the frauds they are."

"Well, your feelings are clear, but we don't use language like that on my show. I am not intellectually impaired. I have to ask, have you received aid from other charities?"

Shayna looks surprised and then uncomfortable. "Of course, Robbie is very sick. I want his short life to be filled with nothing but joy. Do you blame me?"

"Did you have to fill out applications for those charities as well?"

"Yes, what's your point?"

"Each charity has a different application process, correct?"

"Technically, but I was told the Heart Wish Foundation didn't have any solid guidelines."

"Did you read the website before you applied?"

"Of course I did!"

A graphic appears on the screen with the legalese from the Heart Wish Foundation's website which reads, "Any gift given on behalf of the Heart Wish Foundation shall be dispensed at the sole discretion of the Foundation. An application to our program does not guarantee selection."

The program cuts back to Madison. "I'm no lawyer, but it seems clear. The foundation has the right to choose who it gives money to."

Shayna Heywood's face turns red. "That's not fair! They should have given money to my Robbie! I filled out their stupid application and gave them all the information they asked for."

The camera zooms in on Madison "That brings us to another question, Mrs. Heywood. Why exactly is Robert entitled to money from the Heart Wish Foundation or any other charity?"

I clutch Will's hand tightly. "Oh my gosh! Madison is going for the whole chimichanga!"

"Un-freakin'-believable! Shayna's ego is walking right into her trap," Will adds as he gives my hand a squeeze.

Shayna is practically shaking with rage. "Now I know why you only have a podcast instead of being on real network TV. I don't think I've ever met a dumber reporter in my whole life. Look at my son! He's sick and dying. I have to strap him in his wheelchair because he's not even strong enough to sit up. Are you too stupid to put it together? We need the help, you witch!"

Madison pulls out a thick binder and sets it in front of her.

"Mrs. Heywood, I think you and I both know

what's in this binder. I'll give you one more opportunity to tell the truth. It's time for the sake of your son to come clean. Does your son qualify for any of the help you've been asking for? Does he have a terminal nerve disease?"

"How dare you question my integrity? I'm Robbie's mom. I know more about his condition than you will ever know!"

Suddenly, Robert sits up straight in the wheelchair and undoes the straps. "Enough, Mom. The gig is up. You've been busted. We've been busted. Everyone knows now — and I'm relieved. I just want to be a normal kid."

"Robert Shayne Heywood! Shut your mouth. You have no idea all the things I've done for you," Shayna says as she tries to fasten the Velcro again.

Robert blocks her hands and stands up. "No! I won't shut up. You didn't do all this for me. You have told years' worth of lies for yourself. The trips to Disneyland, the hospitalizations, the medical appointments — those were all about you. They were to show the world what a perfect mother you were. What a load of BS! The only reason you got away with it for so long is because I didn't want you to put my little brothers and sisters through all this garbage. Those trips to all the special places you conned people out of, they were only fun for you. They weren't fun for us because we had to pretend I was sick. It's no fun to lie. I'm done. I can't wait to graduate from high school and go to college."

Madison turns to Robert. "You plan to go to college? What do you want to major in?"

He rolls his eyes. "I want to major in psychology. I want to know what causes Munchausen Syndrome by Proxy. I don't want any other kid to go through what I've gone through. I want to protect my siblings."

"I've told you before, I'm not sick!" Shayna Heywood shrieks.

"Yeah, right, Mom. If you're not sick, then you're just a thief. So, whatever! Mr. Kordes, if you can hear this, I'm sorry our family has given your charity a bad name. You don't deserve it. My mom needs some kind of help. But, that's not your fault. I'm sorry she took it out on you."

Madison smiles at Robert. "That was a real stand up thing to say. I invited you on to set the record straight. I think you did just that. Thank you for your time today. I'd like to thank the viewers for tuning in. Join me for my next episode."

Will and I watch with stunned amazement as the screen fades to the closing credits.

Will clears his throat. "Well, I guess that's settled. Everyone told me the Girlfriend Posse has amazing powers, but never in my wildest dreams did I dream of something like that."

"I knew Madison was a phenomenal journalist, but I didn't expect Robert to be the hero of the story. That was legendary," I reply with a grin. " This development ought to take Mallory's exposé on *Word Soup* in a whole new direction."

"I bet. Speaking of that, my disclaimer says the Heart Wish Foundation can help anyone at my sole discretion, correct?"

I nod.

"There's nothing in the fine print which says I have to grant the wish they initially asked for —"

A smile crosses my face as I catch on to Will's train of thought. "When I get out of the hospital, I will email Robert directly and ask him which colleges he would like to visit, and I will offer him a full ride scholarship — complements of the Heart Wish Foundation."

Will high-fives me. "Excellent! It could not have been easy to stand up to his mother. That kind of bravery needs to be richly rewarded. I'd like to meet that young man. Can we make it happen?"

"I'll work on it."

Will takes my iPad away. "You will, but not today. Today, we're going to watch some mindless TV and take a vacation from the world."

I curl into Will's side and rest my head on his chest. "I love it when a plan comes together."

CHAPTER SEVENTEEN

WILL

INSTEAD OF DRIVING BACK to the townhouse, I hit the button on a remote on my keychain and the garage door lifts. So far so good — Mariam is gawking around in amazement when we pull into a spacious garage. Considering where I came from, I'm crazy proud of this space. Most people's garages are filled with clutter, but this one is as neat as a pin. There are storage lockers from floor-to-ceiling.

Like a kid at Christmas, I quickly walk around my car and help her out of the low sports car. "Ready to go in?"

As I help Mariam through the doorway, we walk up a small ramp. "Well, what do you think?" I ask, practically jumping up and down with excitement.

"About what?" she asks.

"The place."

"The wood floors and vaulted ceilings are amazing. I love the marble countertops. I don't think I've ever seen that color before. It's beautiful!"

I let out a deep breath. "Oh, good! I was hoping you would like it. I didn't get a chance to ask you about your favorite colors."

She spins around and looks at me with wide eyes. "Wait a second … This is your house? When did you get a house? I was only in the hospital for four days. How did you get a house?"

"I've been working with Max, an attorney Jeff recommended, for a while. But when you got really sick, I had to put my plans in high gear."

"My fibro fog must be worse than I thought. I don't understand."

"You've mentioned fibro fog before, but you didn't feel up to explaining much."

"Fibromyalgia interferes with the way your nerves interpret information. It can interfere with brain function too. When I'm having a bad flare, it feels like I've taken too much cold medication. My brain doesn't think right. I can't put thoughts together correctly and nothing makes sense. I call it fibro fog. It simply means I'm sorta with it, but not quite."

"So, what's confusing?"

"Why did you have to speed up buying a house because I was in the hospital?"

"Oh, that … Well, honestly… you scared the crap out of me," I admit with a look of chagrin.

"I told you up front that would happen," she answers, sounding defensive.

"Yeah, you did. But hearing about it in the abstract and living through it are two different things. You passed out on the way to the hospital and I couldn't wake you up. It was kind of like when I had seizures as a kid. Now, I know why my mom always freaked out. I've never been so scared in my life."

"Sometimes, when the pain is extreme that can happen. But what does my hospitalization have to do with your new house?"

"I needed a way to keep you safe. Your place has stairs. If you ever passed out on the stairs, you could massively hurt yourself."

Mariam bristles. She struggles to draw a deep breath and stand up straight. "I know you mean well, but you cannot protect me from myself or my disease."

I'm completely baffled.

"You're angry?" I pull out a kitchen chair and sit down. I hang my head in my hands. "I thought you would be happy. No more climbing up and down stairs to do your laundry or to go outside."

"But … Will —" she tries to interject.

"That's not all. There's a large bathtub with therapeutic jets, a sauna, and a hot tub. I put a bench in the shower, and there's a ramp for Maddie and Kiera. I've thought of everything."

"Not quite everything," she mumbles under her breath.

"We could get a dog. I'd like to get a golden retriever."

"That's not what I mean," she replies as she lets out a frustrated breath.

She walks over to the kitchen table and sits in the other chair.

"It's not? What did I miss? Are you a cat person? I

can live with that."

"You're missing the big point here. We don't live together! You didn't ask me to live with you. We've never talked about living together! I'm just your girlfriend. As far as I know, you could have twenty of them. Living together is a big step. People who live together like you're talking about should be in love." As soon as she finishes talking, Mariam covers her mouth with her hand. "Oh my gosh! Forget I said anything. I shouldn't have said all that. Sometimes I'm too honest."

"Honesty is good. I guess I haven't been honest enough."

Mariam gasps and covers her face with her hands. "Geez! I was kidding about the twenty women. If it's true, please don't tell me."

I gently pull her hands away from her face. "Mar, that's not what I meant. You have been my only focus since the day you confronted me in the parking lot of Joy and Tiers."

"Really?"

I kiss the back of her hand. "Why would I look anywhere else? You are beautiful, smart, endlessly fascinating and amazing."

Her nose wrinkles as she struggles to accept my words. "Oh, oka —"

"Wait … I lied."

Mariam nods. "I knew all that had to be too good to be true."

"Hear me out."

Mariam bites her lip but continues to look skeptical.

"I told you that you were my only focus from the

moment we met. But that's not quite right … meeting you inspired me to focus on improving myself. I've been focusing on making Will Kordes someone worthy of the likes of you."

Mariam groans. "Oh my gosh! I must've sounded like a judgmental jerk. I'm so sorry. I was pretty hard on you. I was judging you through the lenses of my past."

"Don't apologize! You gave me a reality check I needed. Before I met you, I was skating through life, counting on a few lucky breaks. I didn't expect very much of myself. I did what was comfortable for me and what made me feel good — but I didn't face the hard things. That took courage I was afraid I didn't have. You showed me I'm strong enough to tackle everything. Regardless of what happens between us, I will forever be grateful."

"This is it … you're giving me the brushoff, aren't you?" Mariam asks tearfully.

"What? No! What makes you think that?" I ask as I stumble over my words. "I must be worse at this than I thought —"

"Will, that's the classic windup to every speech I've ever heard. It goes a little something like this: 'Mariam, I cherish everything you mean to me, but I think we'd really be better off as friends.' Trust me, I've heard a dozen or more variations of that conversation."

"Well, you haven't heard mine!"

"Yeah? Let's hear it."

"Mariam Fischer, the day I was accidentally a jerk and blocked your car with mine was the best day of my life. I wasn't expecting to meet someone who would change everything about me, but you did."

"I did?"

"You did. You turned what was a hobby with a quirky business name into a legitimate business I'm proud of and a foundation I formed to honor my nephew into a bona fide charity with a purpose and a presence other people can understand."

"Anybody would've done that for you."

"No, that's simply not true. I've worked with people for years on my business. None of them helped me build the business like you. In fact, you found a person who was actively working to destroy it."

"I'm so sorry about Steve. He's a jerk!"

"I don't think you understand the full extent of how you've changed me. Before I met you, I was great at faking it. I did just enough to fool people. I was the eccentric guy who invented stuff in my basement like some deranged scientist. But I didn't know how to work my way through a simple lease agreement or contract. I trusted other people to keep me safe. Worse yet, I didn't know how to tell people I needed help. I just pretended I didn't. No one except my sister knew the real me until you. You gave me permission to be me."

"Wow, I'm glad. Your friendship means a lot to me too."

"Remember, I promised you honesty in this conversation. I don't want just friendship out of our relationship. I know I'm your boss and that could complicate things, but somewhere along the way I've fallen in love with you and I can't imagine my life without you."

Mariam's mouth opens and shuts like a guppy gasping for air. "I … I … I don't know what to say. Are you asking me to move in with you, or to marry you, or both?"

"All of it. I want all of it, remember? Plus, a golden retriever," I blurt. *Man! Every time I had one of these conversations in my head, it was a lot smoother. I'm such a dork!*

Mariam swallows hard and gestures around the large kitchen and great space. "Will, I'm at a loss for words. I just got out of the hospital. I wasn't expecting any of this to happen. I need time to think it through once I am feeling stronger."

"Does that mean you're saying no? You won't stay in the guest room?"

"I'll stay. I'm not sure about the rest of it yet."

"Fair enough. I'm a patient man. I can win you over."

"Oh, I have no doubt. The power of Will is a dangerous thing."

"I'm counting on it, but for reinforcement, wait until you see the rest of the hous —"

My phone interrupts our conversation. I look and notice it's Izzy. I answer it and put it on speaker.

"Hey, Izzy! Great choice on the kitchen counters, Mariam loves them."

"I hate to bother you during the big reveal, Mr. K, but I think you need to get back to the office. There's a guy here. He says his name is Norman. He wants to talk to you right away. He won't let me take a message. He says it's personal. I kinda believe him. He looks like an ancient version of you."

Mariam removes the phone from my hand. "We'll be there in a few."

I look at Mariam with haunted eyes. "I never figured they would find him. Now what?"

"You might want to take a few minutes to collect yourself. I recommend a firm handshake followed by a hug. But, that's just me."

"Sounds like a solid plan, let's go face the music."

———•———

As we drive down the two-lane highway back to the headquarters of Hallway Innovations, my hands are shaking and I'm finding it hard to catch my breath. "This is absolutely insane! I've waited almost two dozen years to talk to Norman Kordes. Now that the opportunity is right in front of me, I can't even think of a coherent thing to say. What happened to all those speeches I laid awake at night thinking about?"

Mariam reaches out and squeezes my thigh. "It's okay. You are a completely different person now. You're not the little kid who was worried about keeping food on the table for your mom and sister."

"Am I really? I still worry about them constantly and wonder if I'm good enough. I stress about whether all my success will suddenly disappear and if I'll have to go back to eating mayo sandwiches and begging for odd jobs for a place to stay. What if my dad was right and I really don't have talent?"

"I know you're worried, but I've seen the contract negotiations for your latest device to improve battery life in handheld devices. Independent testing results look phenomenal. You haven't even done a formal presentation of your final product yet and you've got several tech giants fighting over the technology. I don't think there's any danger of you running out of ideas or suddenly becoming a failure."

"Why is this so scary? You're right! I am a grown man with a successful business and an even more successful charity. Why do I feel like a twelve-year-old who has been caught cutting class?"

"I don't know. If anyone should feel awkward, it should be your dad."

My teeth begin to chatter and my hands are trembling so violently I have to pull the car over to the side of the road. I lean forward and rest my head against the steering wheel. "*Kendall!* What am I going to tell my sister? Someone has to tell her dad has popped back into our lives after twenty years. I don't even know where to begin with my mom."

Mariam gets out of the car and walks around to my side. She opens my door and uncharacteristically helps me out of the car. She escorts me to the front of the car and wraps her arms around me in a tight hug. We stand there for several moments as I absorb her quiet strength.

"First, you need to figure out if this is really your dad. We've had more than our fair share of people pretending to be one thing and then turning out to be something entirely different. Let's make sure it's really him before we turn everyone else's life upside down, okay?"

"Oh, right. I don't know why I didn't think of that. You would think I'd be a little more skeptical by now."

Mariam tips her head up and kisses the bottom of my chin. "No worries. That's why you hired the Princesses of Skepticism. You get to stay the King of

Optimism."

"Is that how you see me?" I ask, puzzled.

Mariam shrugs. "I do. You have to be to start a business from scratch and be an inventor of things which have never been created before. You start with dozens and dozens of prototypes, but you never give up until you find a working one. Of course, you have to be the King of Optimism. Otherwise, it would never work. It's perfect. We balance each other."

I place my arm around her waist and walk her back over to the driver's side of my car. "How are you feeling?"

Mariam holds my hand out and watches it shake. "I'm good. I think I'm a little more solid than you at the moment. After all, I've had several days of sleep."

I fish my keys out of my pocket and drop them in her hand. "Good — I need you to drive. I'm a mess. I don't want to die before I see my dad again."

Mariam winks at me as she slides into the driver's seat. "I don't want to die either because I haven't had a chance to tell you I love you, too."

Chapter Eighteen

Mariam

"After our conversation, I'd rather be flying to Rome or the Caribbean. I want to be celebrating the milestone in our relationship not dredging up old history," Will says with a sigh.

"There will be plenty of time for that kind of stuff later. If you don't make peace with your past, you'll never be able to truly move forward with your life. You owe it to yourself. Think of it as setting yourself free."

"We always talked about locating him. I just never thought about what it would feel like when I actually had my hand on the doorknob. This is for Kendall and my mom. Whatever happens, they're my family." Will resolutely opens the door.

As we enter the office, Will is gripping my fingers so tight I'm afraid he might accidentally break them. Izzy stops us as soon as we get inside. "You're not gonna believe this! I think this guy really is your dad. He has pictures of you and Kendall when you guys were kids. One of them is from your fifth birthday party."

Will blows out the breath he's been holding. "Okay, thanks for the heads up." He glances around the office. "Where is he? Don't tell me he already skipped out —"

Izzy shakes her head. "No! He seemed hungry, so I had the place next door deliver some coffee and pastries. Norman is in the conference room waiting for you. He's a sweet old man. He seems like an okay guy — maybe a little confused and sad. Try to be nice, okay Mr. K? You don't know what he's been through."

Will shoots her a tight grin. "I'll give it my best shot. Thanks for keeping him company."

"No biggie, Mr. K."

"I'm not sure I'm ready for this," Will mutters under his breath.

"You can do this. You're great with people, remember?"

"On what planet?" he answers as he gives me the side eye.

"This one!" I insist. "You're great at thinking on your feet. Come on, the anticipation is probably worse than the real thing. Let's get it over with."

Will leads me to the conference room and opens the door. As soon as we see the older man seated at the table, Will exclaims, "Geez-o-Pete! It's like staring into a time machine."

The gentleman stands up and walks towards us. "Not much doubt you're my son, is there, William? You're my spitting image. I looked just like you back in my better days. How is Jennie?"

Will sits down at the conference table. I stop at the coffee machine and pour us both a cup of coffee. I offer to top off Norman's cup, but he covers his cup with his hand and shakes his head. I brush my fingertips across Will's shoulders in a gesture of encouragement before I sit down.

He flashes me a grateful smile before he addresses his father. "Mom lives in Nebraska; exactly where you left her. She hasn't moved or changed her phone number because she was sure you were planning to come back. Dad, you left to get a beer and didn't come back for over twenty years. Where in the heck have you been?"

"It's complicated."

"No kidding, Dad! I was working two or three jobs before I ever set foot in high school just to help Mom keep a roof over our heads. Don't tell me about complicated! I already learned that lesson."

"Look, I'm sorry. I made some terrible mistakes. I promised your mom I would never let alcohol ruin our marriage and then I went and did it. While I was drunk, I got into an accident and scrambled my brains real bad. For a while, I couldn't remember who I was. A police officer was sure I was some homeless dude who had been a confidential informant, and I was too messed up to argue. So I went along. They sentenced me to eight years because I hit a little girl and paralyzed her or something like that. Paid for my mistake with eight years in."

"What do you expect me to say? Congratulations?"

"Yeah, I suppose you could. For the first time in your life, I finally got clean and sober."

Will's face turns red and I feel him getting wound up. I place my hand on his forearm as I lean forward to ask a question, "Norman, congratulations. I'm sure it took a lot of courage and hard work to turn your life around, but that would've been like ten years ago, right? What took you so long to come back?"

Norman looks at me blankly. "I'm sorry, I don't know you. Should I know you?"

"I apologize, I didn't introduce myself. I am Mariam Fischer, William's girlfriend."

"She's much more than that, Dad. Someday, I'm going to marry her."

Norman's gaze travels to my bare fingers. "I don't see no ring on her finger, son. Seems to me you forgot to seal the deal."

"Our lives are a little chaotic right now. We're juggling lots of different things. We're still sorting out logistics," I hasten to explain.

Norman raises an eyebrow in disbelief as he levels a stare at me. "Seems to me you'd want to get your hooks in him as fast as you can. I understand my son is worth a great deal of money."

Will leans back in the leather conference chair and balances it against the wall as he rubs his eyes with the heels of his hands. "Stupid me! I thought you actually came back because you wanted to connect with Kendall and me. I thought you stayed away because you were protecting Mom and the cherished memories you have of us as a family. But I was wrong."

Norman looks crestfallen. "What do you mean?"

"Obviously, you found out about the success of Hallway Innovations. You didn't come back because you missed us or because you love Mom — you came back because I have money. It's as simple as that."

"I know what it looks like, but that's not what happened. I was a terrible dad, I'll give you that. The war messed me up bad. Even when I was around, I wasn't there for you kids. I spent most of my time with you drunk or high. There's no excuse, and I won't even try to give you one. I owed your mom so much more."

"You sure did. It's too bad she couldn't see that. You know she still loves you — probably as much or more than the day she married you?"

Norman looks stunned. "No, I didn't know. I figured she moved on to another guy a long time ago. She should have. Lord knows, she should've. I wasn't worth waiting for — I should've died that day."

"What happened, Norman?" I ask. "Please explain it."

"I was mad at Jennie for something stupid. I think she fixed macaroni and cheese for dinner and I wanted chicken. It was that crazy. I accused her of caring only for the two of you, so I told her I was going out for beer and cigarettes. She told me I'd already had enough to drink. Well … that ticked me off even more. So, I took that little sports car you and I was working on. Only … I was so drunk I forgot the brakes didn't work so great. I drove and drove and drove until it was practically out of gas. I ran right through a stupid stop sign. I hurt a little girl real bad. I don't remember much after that."

Norman leans over and shows me a scar on his head. "They had to put a plate in my head and I had a hundred and fourteen stitches. I spent eight years in the Kansas State penitentiary."

"Kansas!" Will exclaims. "How far did you go to get

beer?"

"A lifetime too far. Do you think you guys can ever forgive me?"

"Norman, you never answered my question. What have you been doing since you got out of prison? Why didn't you go back to Jennie and the kids then?"

Norman hangs his head. "At first, I was on parole and I couldn't leave the state. I went to all sorts of AA meetings to stay sober. I couldn't get a job to save my soul. Nobody wanted to hire an ex-con — especially one convicted of hurting a little girl."

"It's frustrating to try to find work when the odds are stacked against you. I know how that feels," I reply. "How did you finally overcome your choices?"

"My parole officer retired, and I got a new guy who spent some time in the service. He actually gave a rat's butt about what happened to me. He hooked me up with another one of his service buddies who runs a garage in Manhattan, Kansas. So, I've been working for Elroy Jones Motors ever since."

"And you couldn't let us know you were okay? I paid thousands of dollars to look for you. Did you know Kendall lost a son to SIDS? She really could have used your support. She was lost for a long time."

"I had a grandson?"

"Yes, Quinn was beautiful and perfect — and then he was gone. Your daughter was devastated. She quit school and broke off her engagement."

"Oh no! She always loved school, and she always wanted to be married and have tons of babies."

"What about Mom? Did you expect her to simply

forget about you?" Will asks, his agitation clear.

Norman unbuttons the top button on his shirt and rolls up his sleeves in a move I've seen Will do hundreds of times. He swallows hard. "No, I guess not. Although part of me hoped she would — even though my heart would have been crushed if she had. I knew Jennie would have been devastated if she knew I hurt a little girl. She always told me my drinking and drug use would be the end of me someday. She doesn't know how right she was. I'm lucky I didn't kill myself or someone else along the way. I came too freakin' close. By the time I got out, you guys had lived ten years on your own and I was afraid I would disrupt all the progress you all had made without me. I figured you guys had probably built a much better life without me in it."

"Bull pucky!" Will yells as he pounds on the table. "You can't just choose to unlove your family because it's convenient. That's a cop-out."

"You're right. I don't deserve a pass. I handled it all wrong. I'll have to earn back everyone's trust. I won't take it for granted."

Will scrubs his hand down his face. "I can't make any guarantees. I have a lot to think about. Leave your phone number with Mariam. After I've thought about it for a while, I'll get back to you."

"I understand. But just remember, I've always loved you. That hasn't changed."

Will sighs. "It's funny that's not how I remember any of it."

Norman cringes. "That's fair. I deserve that too."

I slide a piece of paper over to Norman. "Please write down your contact information. It's been a long and exhausting day. Thank you for reaching out. We'll be in touch."

Will stands up, extends his hand and shakes his father's hand. I notice he doesn't resist when Norman hugs him.

I breathe a sigh of relief. Perhaps this tangled family mess can be sorted out amicably after all.

———————•———————

This time, it's me who has a horrible case of nerves. Before we reach my parents' front door, I turn around and place my hand in the middle of Will's chest. "We don't have to do this today. You've been through a lot already. I can tell my mom I'm not up to it."

"I'm fine. Your parents are probably worried sick about you since you just got out of the hospital. Besides, I could use a normal family dynamic for once."

I snicker. "I'm not sure you'd call our family normal. If the mood strikes, my parents can fight like hormonal teenagers. Elijah and I don't always get along so well either — although, I have to say he has mellowed quite a bit since he got married."

Will takes a step back. "Do your parents know we're an item or do I need to keep our relationship under wraps?"

"You're silly! I'm a college graduate. I don't have to ask my parents' permission to have a boyfriend. If I'm going to move, I should probably tell people."

"Probably, but maybe not the first time I meet them," Will frets.

I don't want to admit he has a point. That's

precisely what I'm worried about. My dad can be a little overprotective. I shrug nonchalantly. "I wouldn't sweat it. If I know my brother, he's already told them all about you. He seems to be one of your biggest fans, especially after you pulled that epic rescue maneuver at Aidan's place."

Will clears his throat. "I'm not sure my maneuver was so epic. I just picked you up and put you in the back seat of my car and drove you to the hospital. I about hyperventilated on the way there. I probably won't share that part of the story with your parents."

My dad opens the door. "Are you guys planning to stand out on the porch and shoot the breeze all day?"

As we step across the threshold, he takes our coats and hangs them in the closet. When he finishes, he extends his hand to Will. "Hi, I'm Seth. You must be the young man we've heard so much about."

"Seth! I need you to come cut this brisket. I don't want it to get cold."

"Roxanne, do you mind? I'm talking to Mariam and her *chatich*."

Will looks at me blankly. "Trust me, you don't want to know," I mumble under my breath.

I roll my eyes at my dad. "Daddy! Do you have to embarrass Will before we even sit down for dinner?"

"What? Is your boyfriend not a good-looking guy? I do not lie."

Sighing, I give my dad a hug. "No, but Will is so much more than a pretty boy. I wish people understood that."

"*Lib gehat tokhter*, I was just teasing. I meant no

harm."

"Seth, don't be rude! I doubt William speaks any Yiddish. He doesn't know you called Mariam your beloved daughter," my mom chides. She grabs Will's arm and leads him into the kitchen. "Come on in. You must be starving."

"It does smell delicious," Will concedes.

"Mariam, can you and Will set the table while your father cuts the brisket?"

I open the silverware drawer and grab a handful of silverware. When I walk over to the table and set the pile down, Will smacks his forehead.

"What?" I ask, confused by his odd reaction. "It's just silverware. Did you expect us to eat with our hands?"

"That's just the problem; I bought tables, chairs, couches and beds for the new place, but I forgot about all the little stuff like dishes and towels. I guess our new house isn't quite so move-in ready after all."

My face lights up. "Are you serious? Can I decorate the house any way I want? Like with ruffles and bows or lava lamps everywhere?"

A pained look crosses Will's face. "It'll be your place too, do whatever makes you feel comfortable."

"Do you care if I make it a Girlfriend Posse project? It would be the perfect thing to take your sister's mind off her pre-wedding jitters."

Will smiles at me as he pulls his wallet out of his back pocket and hands me his platinum card. "Yeah, that's the perfect plan. You should take Izzy with you. I think she'd have fun hanging out with your group. By the way, when you're buying sheets for my bed, I like flannel sheets. Oregon isn't Nebraska cold, but I still like to be cozy."

I stick my tongue out at him. "I can see we are going to fight over the thermostat. I like to sleep with a fan on."

"Lucky for you the temperature in each room is individually controlled."

My mom and dad set the food on the table and cross their arms as they give us the evil eye. "I don't know, Seth, seems to me Mariam has forgotten to tell us a few things. Do you know what she's talking about?"

My dad shakes his head. "No, I went out for pie with Mariam a couple weeks ago, but even I don't know what she means."

Will gestures toward the table. "Please sit down and I'll be happy to explain."

After everyone settles in, I help myself to some food and pass it around. "This is going to take a bit to explain, there's no need for the food to get cold. Mom, this looks amazing. Thank you so much. Hospital food is such a drag."

My mom slowly inspects me from head to toe. "You look so healthy, I almost forgot you were in the hospital. How are you feeling?"

"I'm great. They put me on different anti-seizure and anti-inflammatory medications to try to control the nerve pain from the fibro. This seems to be a good combination. I'm not as spacey as I was before. I was super frustrated when Will suggested the hospital. You guys know all the nightmarish experiences I've had at the ER. I don't know what miracle Will pulled off, but this time I was treated like gold. They didn't look at me like I was some crazy person or a junkie looking to get a fix."

My mom looks at Will with tears in her eyes. "Thank you so much for caring about my daughter. I worry about her constantly."

"I'm sorry you have to worry about me, Mom. I never wanted it to be this way. I'd give anything for my life to go back to the way it was before."

My mom gets up from the table and comes over to give me a hug. "If I have learned anything over the last few years, it's that you can't turn back time — no matter how hard you wish for it. It is what it is. You just learn to cope the best you can — together. When your dad was hurt, I used to spend a lot of time wishing for the man he used to be. It took me a long time to understand I had to fall in love with the man he is now every single day."

I glance over at my dad. He has worked really hard in physical therapy. Yet, he still has to walk with a cane and he will never get full function back where they damaged his nerves in the attack. Even so, it is clear my mother loves him as much as she did when they first met. My voice catches as I say, "That's unbelievably sweet, Mom."

"You could take some lessons, my stubborn daughter. I think you have to fall in love with yourself every day — even if it's a bad day."

"I know, Mom. It's just hard. I remember what life was like before pain. I wasn't a cranky monster who needed to sleep constantly. I miss that person."

Will leans in and brushes a kiss across my cheek. "I

wish you could see the Mariam I see. Sure, your flares suck. It would be great if the doctors could come up with a way to stop your pain. But, just like you say, I'm more than my good looks, you're more than just your pain."

My dad leans forward and hangs on every word Will utters. "This young man is a smart one. You should pay attention."

"Thank you, sir. Your daughter is brilliant too. She has almost single-handedly organized my business from the ground up and turned my vision into reality. Before she came into my life, I was skating around the edges of success. Every once in a while, I came up with a good invention and made some money. Mariam is the one who turned me into a bona fide business person."

"You know what they say, behind every successful man is a strong woman," my mom says as she walks around and sits back down beside my dad and squeezes his hand.

"That is very true, Roxanne," Will answers with a wide grin. "Mariam has given me an even bigger gift though. She taught me to believe in myself. I'm a better person because your daughter is in my life."

"Mariam, this one is so much nicer than the last one. It's obvious he cares about you and he's taking wonderful care of you," my mom gushes.

Will blushes bright red. "Ma'am, I know you think I'm taking care of your daughter. The truth is, keeping me safe is probably a tougher job."

I can see my dad's overprotective antenna shoot straight up. "What are you saying? Is all the stuff they said on the news about you true?"

"No, Dad! Did you see the interview with the family? The son busted his mother. Their whole scam fell apart right in the middle of a live interview with Madison. Will is an honorable guy. My heart is safe with him. This time, I didn't fall in love with a jerk," I insist.

"Mari, are you saying William is your Seth?" my mom asks in a reverent tone.

My stomach tightens and my palms start to sweat. "You guys know me. I've had really bad luck. I'm scared to trust my heart. So, I'm taking it really slow. Will bought a brand-new house because he was afraid I would fall on the stairs in the townhouse if I had a really bad flare. I'm staying in the guest room."

My dad nails Will with a shrewd look. "You okay with this arrangement? A man doesn't go around buying houses for a houseguest."

"I'm a straight shooter. I won't lie to you. I love your daughter. Honestly, I think I started falling in love with her from the moment she started chewing me out on the day we met. But I don't think she feels the same way."

"I sympathize. Sometimes when you know, you just know."

"Right? So, I'll wait until Mariam believes in love again."

My mom wipes away tears. "I hope for your sake, it doesn't take too long for my daughter's hope to heal."

I look at my mom quizzically. "Don't you mean heart, Mom?"

My mom shakes her head adamantly. "No, Mariam, I said exactly what I meant. Those bozos before never got close enough to you to break your heart. They never truly crushed your heart — only your hope for the future. Seems to me you've got that sitting right beside you. It's up to you to decide whether you want to live in the past or in the future."

CHAPTER NINETEEN

WILL

"WHATEVER YOU DO, PLEASE don't tell me the two of you are fighting!" Kendall exclaims as she rushes into our kitchen and sets her shopping bags on the floor. She pauses to give Mariam a hug before she sees the spread on the kitchen table. "Oh! You made us breakfast. Jameson will be happy. He is tired of diet food. But … you know how it is. I'm afraid to walk past the donut rack in the grocery store for fear I'll gain weight and not fit into the dress Jordan made."

"Relax, Sis." I walk over to the stove and show her the container of egg substitute. "I used low-cal eggs in your veggie omelet."

Jameson peers down at the plates. "I know I gotta look good for the wedding pictures, but I need a little something more. Veggies won't cut it."

I walk over to the oven and pull out a pan of bacon. "Ta-da! Got you covered!"

Kendall's eyes widen. "Since when do you know how to cook?"

I put my arm around Mariam's waist. "I have an excellent teacher. Did you know they have whole networks devoted to cooking shows? I have a brand new hobby now. Cooking competitions are strangely addicting."

Jameson chuckles. "I see you've settled into homeownership just fine. Soon you'll be watching other people buy houses on TV."

"That's a thing?"

Mariam, Kendall and Jameson simultaneously answer, "Yes."

I look at Mariam. "Should we watch?"

Again, all three of them vigorously shake their heads and reply, "No!"

"I'm sure you didn't invite us over for breakfast to talk about TV. What's up?" My sister asks as she carries the plates over to the kitchen table. "You sounded so serious over the phone."

"Well … how flexible are your wedding party and guest list?"

Out of nowhere, Kendall's small fist flies up and hits my bicep. "I knew it! You changed your mind about being in my wedding. You're supposed to be my best man. Mariam is my maid of honor. You can't flake on me. The wedding is in nine days."

"Kendall, listen —"

"You have to walk me up the aisle with Mom. You promised. That's what family does."

"I know I did, but something has come up and it might change your plans."

"What could possibly change my plans? I've been

waiting to get married since I was a little girl. My wedding is less than two weeks away."

"Kendie, I wasn't always your first choice to walk you down the aisle, was I?"

She shakes her head. "No, I always figured Dad would do it. But we all know how that dream turned out. He's long gone. As far as I know, he's probably de—"

Kendall's speech dies mid-sentence as she catches my expression. "Holy cow! Are you saying what I think you're saying?"

I nod. "Norman Kordes is alive, presumably doing well, and asking for forgiveness."

"Wait! What? When? How? What happened?" Kendall peppers me with questions as quickly as they come to mind.

"I don't know much. I think he found me because of all the media attention surrounding the Heart Wish Foundation. Honestly, if it wasn't for the fact that he looks like the spitting image of me, I wouldn't believe this was true. He just showed up at my office. I had no idea he was coming. I have little doubt he's legit. He knows too much private stuff only we know about."

Jameson leans forward. "Still could be an elaborate catfishing hoax. You should see some of the cases Tristan and I handle. These people go deep undercover."

"It's him. I'll never forget his voice. It haunts my dreams," I answer as my stomach lurches.

"How is he?" Kendall asks tentatively.

"Do you mean is he a mean-tempered drunk who

can't hold his tongue?" I reply sardonically.

Kendall cringes. "I guess I try to suppress those memories of him in favor of happier times, but yeah — I suppose that's what I'm asking."

"We didn't meet for very long. I didn't trust myself to stay civil. But he seemed contrite and clean and sober for a change."

Kendall reaches over and hugs Jameson. She buries her face in his chest. "I'm so torn! This could change everything … or it could change nothing. I don't know what to do."

Jameson strokes my sister's hair for a few moments. "What does Jennie say about all this?"

"Nothing yet. She doesn't know."

Kendall lifts her head. "Mom should have the final vote. Her life will be the most impacted by our decision."

"I think this is something she'll have to do in person. She needs to be able to measure his sincerity," Jameson advises.

"First-class tickets it is. I was planning to fly Mom out for your wedding anyway. So, now she'll arrive a few days ahead of time."

"I know Mom has been expecting Dad to walk in the door for more than twenty years. But, deep down inside I don't know which outcome is best for her."

"Having met the new improved version of Dad, I'm not sure either. Maybe love conquers all or maybe too much time has passed to make it work."

"I guess the only way we'll find out is to reintroduce our parents."

It's only been a few months since I've seen my mom, but it feels great to give her a bear hug. You know what else feels great? Showing off my beautiful girlfriend. I told Mom all about Mariam the last time I was home, but I think my mom suspected I was wildly embellishing some casual dating story to make her happy. To be fair, I've been known to pull those shenanigans before. My mom has always been so dedicated to Kendall and me settling down and giving her grandchildren, I may have given her the illusion that some of my previous relationships have been more serious than they really were. But this time, it's the real deal and my happiness is written all over my face.

We collect my mom's luggage and drive to a nearby restaurant. After we order our food my mom looks around the table with concern. "Kendall, why am I here so early? My boss isn't happy with me. I had to tell him I had a family emergency. Do I have a family emergency? Are you calling off the wedding?"

Kendall shakes her head. "No, Mom, I'm a little stressed out, but I'm still getting married."

She turns to Mariam. "What about you? Am I going to be a grandmother soon?"

Mariam lets out a startled burst of laughter. I blush clear to the roots of my hair. "Mom! Some manners might be nice. You just met Mariam."

Mariam takes a sip of soda and collects herself before addressing my mother. "Mrs. Kordes, it's okay. I understand, I'd be confused too. Your son is a great guy and he's my best friend. But we're not making babies yet. I've got some serious health issues which may mean that's not a good idea. But either way, that's not why you're here early."

"Oh my gosh! Is somebody dying?"

My jaw tightens and I seethe with frustration, but it's all aimed inward. I can't believe I've screwed this up so badly. "No, Mom, I don't think anyone is dying. There's no easy way to break this news. So I'll just come right out and tell you. Remember a few weeks back when that crazy lady was threatening to sue me and the Heart Wish Foundation was all over the national news?"

"Oh, don't tell me she went through with her whackadoodle scheme —"

"No, thank goodness her so-called 'case' collapsed like a cheap suit as soon as she was challenged by a reporter who knew the facts. The publicity had another side effect, though."

"Mom, Daddy found us," Kendall interjects, unable to contain her excitement.

"Are you sure it's him? I've never been lost. I stayed in the same place for over two decades. If Norman wanted to find me, he should've just come home," my mom replies through tears. "I've been waiting forever."

Kendall takes my mom's hands and clasps them in her own. "I talked to him on the phone the other day. There were issues."

"'*Issues*'? I bet. Was she blonde or brunette … or were the 'issues' the liquid kind?"

Whoa! This is not the response I expected from my mom. She always paints such a rosy picture of their marriage, sometimes I wonder whether I imagined all the bruises, yelling and discord I remembered as a kid. Maybe my mom didn't spend all these years waiting for my dad to come back like some knight in shining armor, maybe she was too frightened to leave. My heart drops into my stomach. What have we done by re-opening the lines of communication? What if my dad hasn't changed at all?

Kendall gasps. "Mom, if Dad acts like a jerk, you don't have to ever see him again. We just thought you missed him."

My mom throws her hands up in the air. "I do! Or, I miss the person I married. The guy he was before he went off to the stupid war. The man who courted me before he started drinking is the man I fell in love with. I don't know who Norman is now. If he's like he was when we first met, maybe I still love him. If he's the monster he was when he disappeared, he can just stay gone."

Jameson clears his throat softly. "I don't know if this will add to your confusion or help alleviate it. Before Kendall contacted Norman, Identity Bank West did a background check to confirm he is who he says he is. It appears he has undergone a fair amount of counseling lately."

My mom's jaw drops open. "I thought all that information was confidential."

"It is. However, your husband willingly provided his information to our investigator. It seems he has been working hard to put his past behind him and he's become a mentor to other people who are struggling with post-traumatic stress disorder and drug and alcohol addiction," Jameson explains.

"How do I know if I can trust him? That hasn't worked out so well before," my mom challenges with a teary shrug.

"I suppose you don't, really. Only you can decide if it's worth the risk to find out if he's telling the truth."

A ghost of a smile crosses my mom's face. "If I don't give him a chance to at least state his case, I'll always wonder what could have been."

I pull out my cell phone and bring up Norman's phone number. "Okay, I'll see what I can do about making it happen."

With her hand shaking, my mom reaches out and touches my arm. "Can it be today? I'm afraid if I wait too long, I'll lose my nerve. You guys have to stay with me though. I still don't know if this is a good idea. It's been a long time since he's seen me. I'm afraid he'll be disappointed."

Mariam smiles at my mom. "Jennie, you are one of the most naturally beautiful women I've ever seen. I can't imagine your husband could possibly be disappointed in what he sees."

"Aren't you sweet? No wonder my son clearly loves you. *Husband* ... I've been single for so long I sometimes forget I actually have one. Okay, let's go talk to this guy who claims to still be in love with me after all these years. This ought to be interesting."

CHAPTER TWENTY

MARIAM

JENNIE DELICATELY DABS AT her lips with a napkin and then pats her short gray hair nervously. "If you two will excuse me, I want to take a few moments to freshen up before the men get back with Dad."

"Go right ahead, Mom," Kendall says as she stands up to let Jennie out of the booth. Anxiously, she watches her mom walk toward the restroom. When her mother is out of sight, Kendall checks the time on her phone for what seems like the hundredth time. "Oh Geez! How long is it going to take them to go get Norman?"

"Relax, you know Will. He probably got distracted by something."

Kendall lowers her voice and moves closer. "I can't relax. If this reunion blows up in our faces, it will ruin my whole wedding. I don't want my mom to be a crying mess when she watches her only daughter get married, know what I mean?"

"I get it," I murmur.

"No, I don't think you understand. My whole life I grew up believing everything in my life would be perfect if only my dad was around."

"I think most little girls feel that way about their dads. It's only natural, how could it not be?"

"I suppose so, but it was different with me. At first, we thought he was coming back right away. When he didn't, we had to figure out how to cope. When there wasn't enough money to have birthday parties or go to camp, it was always because my dad was gone. My mom would always insist it would be better when he came back. She always acted as if he was off on some grand adventure. Even after all he put her through, she never seemed angry — at least never that I saw. Maybe Will witnessed a different side of things than I did, but for me it didn't seem any different from the stories she told about the times he was away at war."

"Maybe that's what she had to tell herself to stay sane. I can't imagine what it must've been like for her. One day, you think your life is one way and then your husband announces he's going out for beer and never comes back? It must have shaken everything she thought she knew about herself."

Kendall lets out a heavy sigh. "It changed us all more than I want to admit. I'm lucky I found someone as accommodating as Jameson who was willing to stick with me while I worked through all my fears. Even though I always believed things would be better if my dad ever came back into our lives, now I'm not so sure. What if he ruins everything on our special day? Jameson has been waiting so patiently for things to settle down and me to get it together."

"Nothing your dad can do will tarnish the love story

between you and Jameson. It belongs to you. You've been to enough weddings around here to know they rarely go according to script."

"That's true! Remember when everybody crammed in Mallory's hospital room for Mindy and Elijah's wedding?"

"Yes!" I shriek so loud the other people in the laid-back diner turn their heads to watch us. "Their ceremony was still incredibly romantic even though nothing went as it was planned. So, we're going to have to hold on tight and see what happens. Who knows? It could be something epically beautiful and just what your mom always hoped for."

Jennie walks up behind Kendall and places her hand on Kendall's shoulder. "Oh honey, are you fretting over my reunion with your dad?"

A tear slides down Kendall's face. "Little bit, Mom." Kendall wipes her tears away with a napkin. "Don't mind me, cocktail napkins stress me out these days. You should've seen me at the floral shop trying to pick out my bouquet. I was a blubbering mess. I'm just afraid Daddy will upset you after you flew all this way to see me get married."

"Kendie, do you honestly think it would be the first time your father upset me? I'm a big girl. I spent twenty-plus years getting strong and tough. If he decides to be a creep, I'll tell him to hit the highway. I've already proven I can survive without him."

"Are you sure?" Kendall presses.

"Yeah, and after I get all this sorted, I can finally move out here where you guys are. As generous as Will is with airfare, it's inconvenient to live in the middle of nowhere."

Kendall stands up and hugs her mom. "That would be great. I miss you so much. Oregon is beautiful. I think you'd love it here."

The bell above the door chimes and every person in the restaurant seems to freeze in anticipation. The three of us stand and face the door as we link our hands and hold our breath with silent hope. The door swings wide and the trio of men enter. Under any circumstances, this group would make a heck of an impression, but the emotionally charged atmosphere makes them seem like heroes from a vintage Hollywood western.

"My goodness, he is still the most handsome man I've ever laid my eyes on," Jennie murmurs as she fans herself. "I don't know how this is possible, but he looks better today than he looked decades ago when he left."

"You're not so bad yourself, Jennie. I could definitely see where your children get their stunning good looks," I comment under my breath.

For several moments, Norman simply drinks in the sight of Jennie as he blinks away tears. He pinches the bridge of his nose and tries to disguise his tears. "Oh Jen, I have so many things to say to you and at this moment I can't think of any. I'm sorry. Everything I did to you was wrong. You did nothing to deserve what I did to you … or the kids. I wish I could erase all the pain I've caused. I'm sorry for the choices I made, and the destruction I left behind."

Norman takes a deep breath and opens his arms wide.

Everyone in the restaurant looks over at Jennie to see what she plans to do. I can feel her tremble. I can't tell if she's shaking from anticipation or frustration.

Jennie takes a tissue out of her pocket and wipes her eyes. "Darn it, Norman Earl Kordes!"

Norman sways at the impact of her words.

"If you'd been half as good at apologies back in the day, we could've avoided a world of hurt. You practically destroyed me. I don't know if I'll ever forgive you for what you did to our children. You scarred them. You know that, right? You changed who they are."

"I know, Jennie. I have no excuses. I screwed up. I'd like a chance to prove I can do better. I'm fourteen years, five months, seven days clean and sober."

"That's a lot," Jennie replies with a shaky smile.

"Thank you. I still work at it every day, but I'm trying to make up for some very bad decisions in my past. I want you to be proud of me."

"You still care what I think?"

"With every beat of my heart. I fell out of love with myself for a while, but I never ever fell out of love with you," Norman insists.

Jennie walks into his outstretched arms. "All I can say is you better not be lying to me, Norman Kordes. I tried for years to get over you and to forget you ever existed. The funny thing is, I never fell out of love with you either. I'm willing to give you another chance. Please don't break my heart again. I don't think I'm strong enough to survive it a second time."

"It crushed me when I broke it the first time, I have no intention of hurting you again." Norman leans down and tenderly kisses Jennie as if there isn't an audience of restaurant patrons hanging on his every word.

After a couple of moments, Will taps his father on the shoulder. "I hate to break this reunion up, but we have to get you fitted for a tuxedo ASAP. You have a daughter to walk down the aisle. You ready for that, Dad?"

"Don't I have to chase him out of her room first and make a few general threatening statements about how he needs to treat her right and all that jazz?" Norman asks as he gives Jameson the once over.

"Daddy! Jameson and I have been together for years. You're a little late to the game. You're just in time for the party now."

"Sounds good to me as long as your mom saves me a dance."

Jennie blushes and curtsies. "Count on it, Mr. Kordes."

<hr>

"What are you doing here? I thought you would be getting ready for the big day. Don't you have maid of honor duties to do?" Izzy asks as she lets herself into the office and sees me sitting behind the desk.

"I do, but that's not until later today. I figured I'd process some last-minute paperwork. The Henderson family needs some help to save their house. It can't wait."

"Cool beans! I'm positive Mr. K would want me to remind you you're supposed to be on vacation, though."

I smirk. "Uh-huh, he can tell me himself when he comes out of his workshop."

"Seriously? He butt-dialed me last night at eleven-thirty p.m. He was confused when he woke me up. When I asked him what he was working on, he said he couldn't tell me. He gave me some mumbo-jumbo about secret military applications."

I roll my eyes. "I know. I've stopped asking. I know it has something to do with helping to find missing soldiers, but other than that, he can't tell me anything."

As soon as Izzy boots up her computer, it beeps. She clicks on the application to answer it. "Hallway Innovations, good morning, Mr. Macklin. What can I do for you?"

"Good morning, Izzy. I know it's early in Oregon, but is Mr. Kordes around?"

Izzy looks over with a panicked expression.

I walk over to stand in front of Izzy's computer in view of the WebCam. I'm surprised to see both Isaac and Tristan. "Morning, gentlemen. I'll have to go get him. Will is probably working with his headphones in. He tends to ignore the intercom when he's working on a project. Is this a private meeting, or do you want us all there?"

Isaac smiles at me. "This is a case update resulting from your hard work. I think everyone should be there."

"Izzy, can you transfer the video call to the conference room? I'll go get Will."

Izzy looks up at the screen. "Okay, sorry for the wait, sir. I'll be with you in a moment. I have to boot up the computer in the conference room."

"No rush. We have been so busy this morning, we haven't even had a chance to stop for a sip of coffee," Isaac assures us.

I slide my feet into my clogs and sprint down the hallway to the workshop. When I skid to a stop in the doorway and knock harder than I intend to, Will looks up with a concerned expression. "Are you sick?"

"No, I'm fine. Isaac and Tristan need to talk to us ASAP. They're waiting on a video call."

Will turns a little gray. "Yikes! If they're both on the line, this can't be good."

"I didn't get that impression. But, I guess it's possible I misunderstood."

Will takes off his headphones and powers down his computer. "Let's go. We can't figure it out from here."

When we enter the conference room, Tristan, Izzy, and Isaac are laughing. "Did we miss something?" I ask.

"Izzy was telling us what a decent guy Robert actually turned out to be," Tristan answers. "I'd love to be a fly on the wall when he finds out Heart Wish plans to give him a full ride to college even after all the garbage his mom pulled."

"We're still working with our legal team to make sure we can do it in a way that ensures the rest of his family has no chance of getting their hands on the money."

"Smart move," Tristan concedes.

"Speaking of keeping money out of the hands of dishonest people, that's why we called," Isaac adds.

Will looks like Isaac just sucker punched him. "No freakin' way! There is another thief in my inner circle?"

Isaac shakes his head. "No, I'm so sorry. I wasn't clear. This is good news. There is no new thief. My colleagues caught Steve Banfield red-handed today. He is in federal custody facing a slew of charges."

"What do you mean, they caught him red-handed?"

Tristan leans forward in his chair. "It seems your friend Steve had a little more than run-of-the-mill jealousy. He was trying to be you. Steve posed as you online using one of your pictures and purchased a vintage Shelby. When he traveled to Texas to retrieve the car, the seller knew Steve was a fraud. I guess you've had dealings with Mr. Houser in the past?"

"Mmm-hmm, my 1967 Chevrolet Corvette Coupe. Did Leap'n Larry call the cops?"

Isaac leafs through a folder on his desk. "From what I understand, your friend was crafty enough to get him to sign a piece of paper using your signature. Then, he took him on a tour of his garage till law enforcement showed up. It must've been a beautiful thing."

Will snickers. "If I recall correctly, Leap'n Larry was a former bailiff. He must've gotten a kick out of that."

Isaac smiles nostalgically. "I imagine so. Doesn't matter how long you've been retired, once you've been involved in the justice system, it always feels good to get a bad guy."

Will shakes his head. "I never in a million years figured Stevo would do something like this."

Izzy pipes up. "I know it's hard Mr. K. Just because someone you trusted turned out to be a jerk, it doesn't mean you are too. It took me a long time to sort that out."

"Thanks, Iz, I'll try to remember that."

CHAPTER TWENTY-ONE

WILL

"You are the most exquisite woman I have ever met in my whole life," I say as I take in Mariam's artful ruby red sheath dress. When she makes a slow turn in front of me, I have to catch my breath when I see her bare back exposed in the cleverly classy, yet daring, design.

Mariam blushes as she carefully pats her elaborate updo. "Thank you. I think Jordan did the impossible. I feel beautiful for a change."

I pull her close as I bend to kiss her bare shoulder. "See, you have it all wrong. You are beautiful every day, whether you wear this or a baggy sweatshirt. It makes no difference. Your beauty is soul deep. It is part of who you are. Your kind of beauty allows you to see a guy like me and find the real person under all the flash and love me anyway."

Mariam waves her hands in front of her face. "Oh, please stop. I can't cry before we have pictures. Donda told us all she didn't have time to redo everyone's makeup."

I kiss her shoulder one more time. "Okay, I promise to be good. Let's go see what everyone else is up to."

I place my arm around Mariam's waist and we walk into the refurbished barn.

My sister is an interesting study in contrasts. Her makeup is much darker than usual and her hair is curled, braided and swept up on the top of her head. Yet, she is wearing jeans with holes worn through the knees. She is wearing one of Jameson's chambray shirts which dwarfs her. Even so, she looks happy and at peace as Justice Gardner runs through the ceremony prep.

Justice Gardner looks down at the wedding party. "I understand there's been a change in the order of things, is that correct?"

My dad puffs out his chest and straightens his bow tie. "Yes, Sir-ee, I'll be walking my gorgeous daughter down the aisle, just like it should be. I've wanted to do this ever since she was a little girl."

My stomach lurches when I hear my dad say those words. I start to sweat and my mouth turns dry. Reversing course, I turn and leave the barn, taking Mariam with me.

She glances up, clearly confused, but she walks quietly beside me. Once we are outside, I walk toward a bench in the rose garden and sit down. My knees are visibly shaking. I take off my tuxedo jacket and place it on the bench behind Mariam.

"How can I help?" Mariam removes a tissue from her cleavage area and hands it to me. I love that she didn't even bother to ask me if something is wrong. She just knows.

"It's probably stupid. But I'm not okay with what

my dad is doing."

"Walking Kendall down the aisle?" Mariam asks, befuddled.

"I know it sounds ridiculous and petty, but Norman hasn't earned the right! Where was he when she was learning to ride her bike? I'll tell you where — he was at the bar. Where was he when she was trying to pass Algebra? Gone! My dad — you know the one so proud of his daughter, ready to step up and take all the credit — he went out to get beer and didn't come back for twenty years. Oh yeah, he was gone when Kendall planned to marry herself a guy who couldn't handle the loss of his child and left her to deal with all the grief by herself. Where was he then? Wasn't so proud to be a dad when the times were tough. Yeah, I'm ticked off. There's more to being a dad than showing up for the pictures."

"I agree. I suspect Kendall probably does as well. She's probably stuck between reality and not wanting to make a scene. I was with her the other day when we all went to the salon to be beautified. Your mom is floating on a cloud. She's like a teenager who's dating for the first time. Kendall doesn't want to upset their reunion."

"Why couldn't he find us next month?" I grouse. "He's going to ruin everything."

Mariam runs her fingers down my jaw. "I'm sorry. I'd be angry too."

I flex my fingers and clench my fists repeatedly as I try to calm down. "I don't know if I'm a good enough liar to pull this off. Kendie will know something is off."

"Will, just feel what you feel. You don't need to apologize for your emotions. Just remember, Norman has only been back a few days. Kendall knows who's been there for her every day. She won't forget who loves her. One walk down the aisle will not wipe out your history."

I lean over and carefully brush a kiss across Mariam's cheek. "I'm so glad you're smarter than me. You're right, this day is about my gorgeous sister. It's merely an accident of fate that my dad happens to be here. He really does make my mom happy. So, I guess I better learn to live with it."

Mariam smiles. "Buck up, GQ. Love is in the air. Besides, you owe me another dance or two."

I try not to fidget as we stand at the back of the barn waiting for the ceremony to start. Mariam leans over and straightens my tie. "How are you feeling about things?" she whispers.

"Surprisingly chill. The guys played video games while you were taking pictures and getting ready. That helped."

"There's been a slight change of plans. Just follow your mom's lead. I'll catch up with you in a bit," Mariam promises mysteriously.

Aiden and Mindy start to play the wedding march on the acoustic guitar. I hold my breath as my father takes my sister's arm and walks down the aisle. I blow out my breath as my heart catches. My sister looks like she belongs in some magazine spread. Her long veil is trailing behind her. Through the transparent netting, I see the angel wing tattoo she got to commemorate Quinn's brief life. It's a tribute to my sister's amazing love story that Quinn's existence has not been forgotten as she moves on to her new life.

My mom appears beside me and puts her hand through the crook of my elbow and urges me to follow Norman and Kendall. Puzzled, I look down at her and then back at Mariam. Mom smiles at me and starts to walk forward. I plaster a grin on my face as if I know what's going on. Everywhere I look, I see cell phones and cameras. I hope I don't look as confused as I feel.

After Kendall and Dad get halfway down the aisle, he gives Kendall a brief hug and sits down. Mom lets go of my arm and walks to one side of Kendall and gestures for me to stand on the other. Kendall hands Mom her bouquet of flowers and places her arms around our waists. Together, we walk up the aisle like the Three Musketeers we've always been.

When we reach the front of the barn, Kendall lifts her veil for a moment. Mom and I each plant a kiss on a cheek. Kendall tearfully says, "I love you guys. Thank you for making this day possible."

Mom hands Kendall her bouquet. "You have incredible strength, you would have made it here without me."

"Says you," Kendall argues.

"Go marry your Prince Charming, you deserve it, Sis."

I'm close enough to Jameson to watch him struggle to hold his emotions. He takes a deep breath and wipes away tears with the pads of his thumbs. Toby takes a tissue from Brynley and hands it over to his brother.

"I've got smelling salts if you need those," he offers.

"You think you're funny, but Kendall is gorgeous

enough to knock me off my feet, so keep 'em handy."

Mariam walks up behind me and takes my hand. As Kendall takes her place next to Jameson, we walk up to the front of the barn and stand next to Toby and Brynley. Mom stops to take a picture of us before she sits down next to Dad. She takes his hand in hers and lays her head on his shoulder.

Justice Gardner steps up to the mic. "Good afternoon, friends and family of Kendall Kordes and Jameson Payne; they're honored you chose to be part of the celebration today. Their story is very much about love lost and found. There are many people here today who are here because these two fell in love. So, today we celebrate not only their story but the impact they've had in the world."

Jameson turns to face Kendall. With great care, he moves the veil away from her face and drapes it back over her head. The audience laughs when his cufflink catches on the edge of her veil when he tries to pull away.

"Ever since the two of you met, you've always been inseparable from my sister," I joke.

Mom steps forward and helps extract Jameson from Kendall's veil and everyone breathes a sigh of relief. He hands the bouquet of flowers to Mariam and interlaces his fingers with Kendall's.

"I gotta be honest with you. When Tristan sent me all the way to Oregon from Florida to fix what I thought would be a simple computer virus, I thought my boss had a few screws loose. After all, he took me off a priority job to get me here."

In the audience, I can see Tristan smirk and roll his

eyes as he clears his throat.

"I've never been so happy to be wrong in my life. But see, I wasn't just wrong about the computer virus and Tristan's state of mind, I was wrong about you. When we first met, I was dead set sure you and the work you did with Locate My Heart was a complete fraud. I wasn't nice about it either. I deserved to be shown the door and kicked in the pants on the way out, but that's not what you did. You showed me love and compassion and tried to understand where my pain was coming from. When you figured it out, you worked night and day to fix it. As a result, you found my brother and brought him home. I never expected to trust anyone again and I certainly never expected to fall in love, yet here I am. You not only found my lost brother, you helped me find myself."

"I'm so glad those idiots tried to take over my computer system," Kendall whispers. "I was lost that day too. I was lost in the past. You didn't know it then, but I was running from a pain so deep I thought I would never recover. When Quinn died from SIDS, my heart broke. I thought if I helped enough families reunite, I might find the answer to my never-ending pain. It turned out the answer was opening my heart to love again. Your love gave me hope."

Justice Gardner turns to Jameson. "Do you, Jameson Payne, promise to love Kendall Kordes during periods of illness and wellness, and in abundance and poverty? Do you promise to cling to each other tightly when all seems lost?"

Jameson smiles tenderly at Kendall. "We've had a rough road to get here, but I've been waiting a really long time to say, I do."

Justice Gardner nods. "Very good." He turns to my sister. "Do you, Kendall Kordes, promise to love Jameson Payne during periods of illness and wellness, and in abundance and poverty? Do you promise to cling to each other tightly when all seems lost?"

Kendall nods enthusiastically. "I do."

Toby steps up on stage. Kendall looks completely baffled.

Toby speaks into the mic. "I know you think you're doing a unity candle ceremony here. We decided to add a surprise twist to it."

Two women step forward. "Because you helped Bethany find her missing son after my mentally ill relative snatched him when my adoption fell through, Bethany became a surrogate mother for my husband and me. We now have a beautiful daughter. We owe our friendship and family to you."

Kendall tears up. "I know I wasn't the only one who had a hand in that miracle."

Bethany steps forward to the microphone. "No, you weren't, but you saved Archer and made it possible for us to help another family, just as you have done for countless other families."

Toby moves toward the microphone. "You convinced people to look for me when everyone else had given up. I'm so glad you'll be my sister-in-law. So, the audience is filled with coworkers and families you and my brother have helped over the years. They all have special candles which are lit in your honor. This is the unique unity ceremony. When you guys go back to look at your wedding video, you can see all the people you've helped. It's a visual representation of the power of love."

Kendall and Jameson turn around and face the audience where dozens and dozens of little candle lanterns are being held up in the air.

Jameson looks back on stage at his brother. "You are the best. Love you, man."

Kendall dabs at her eyes. "This is unbelievable. You guys are amazing. Thank you so much for coming."

The audience stands up and claps for several minutes. When it dies down, Justice Gardner looks down at his notes and then up at my sister. "After that, I seem to have lost my place. You two have rings to exchange, correct?"

"We do. Will is in charge of those." She looks over at me. "William Benjamin Kordes, don't you dare pull any funny business! Someday, I'll be in your wedding and you know what they say about payback."

I hold my hands up in protest. "Who me? Would I do something like that to you?"

I'm not sure what it means that most of the people present at my sister's wedding roar with laughter and answer with a resounding, "Yes!"

Maddie wheels over in her wheelchair carrying a little ring bearer pillow on her lap. "Mr. Will says these are your wedding rings."

Much to my relief, Kendall and Jameson bust out laughing when they see what I've tied to the pillow.

Kendall tilts the pillow to show the audience the Mickey and Minnie Mouse rings. In my defense, they are stunning diamond and sapphire encrusted rings, they are just not the simple understated rings Jameson and my sister picked out.

Jameson clears his throat. "Well, I have to say, William, these rings are very … umm … you. Thank you."

Kendall looks toward her maid of honor frantically. "Mariam, you can rescue us from my brother's crazy plan, right?"

Mariam grins as she reaches into the pocket of her dress. "Of course, it's all in a day's work." She hands the new rings over to Justice Gardner.

"What's wrong? Don't you trust me with them?" I tease.

"Mr. Will, I think you blew it," Maddie advises. "You may never get to be in a wedding again."

Justice Gardner swallows a grin. "Is everyone ready to proceed?"

He hands the rings to them and says, "A ring is a visible token of your unending love and commitment for each other and a reminder that your spouse is always by your side."

Kendall holds out her hand for Jameson. Judge Gardner asks, "Kendall do you accept this ring from Jameson?"

"I do," she replies as she admires the silver band with a thin rope of diamonds wound through it.

Justice Gardner continues, "Jameson do you accept this ring from Kendall?"

Jameson nods. "I do." When he sees the gleaming silver band he smiles. "I like this one a lot better than your brother's choice."

"It has been a great honor to watch your love story

grow over the years and to welcome the two of you into our community. As evidenced by this beautiful ceremony, the two of you have done a profound amount of good in a few short years, we are privileged to count you as friends. So, by the power vested in me as a former member of the Oregon judiciary, I pronounce you husband and wife. You may kiss your bride, Mr. Payne."

"Not a moment too soon," Jameson replies as he cups Kendall's face and kisses her so thoroughly, I am convinced he forgot any of us are in the room.

CHAPTER TWENTY-TWO

MARIAM

"No, no, no, no!" I murmur to myself as I watch Heather unveil the spectacular castle cake. This can't be happening. *Not here. Not now.* My bowels twist and I kick off my high heels and run to the restroom.

Thank goodness no one is around as I deal with one of the most unpleasant and unpredictable side effects of my fibro flares. Will is probably wondering where I am. I did not expect to spend my time as a maid of honor camped out in the restroom.

I glance at myself in the mirror as I'm washing my hands. It's a good thing we took pictures earlier. All of Donda's artfully applied makeup can't disguise my paleness. When I rejoin the party and reluctantly put my shoes back on, Mindy quietly walks up beside me. "You need to tell Will what's going on."

I shake my head. "I'm fine. He's having a good time. I don't want to bother him. This is a once-in-a-lifetime moment for him."

Mindy studies me with concern. "Are you sure?"

"I'm sure. I think the worst has passed," I assure her with far more confidence than I have.

Will sees me from across the room. His smile is enough to melt my heart. He picks up two tall champagne flutes from a tray and heads in my direction.

When he reaches me, he hands me a glass. "I brought you cranberry sparkling cider. I have apple if you want to trade. Kendall is cutting the cake now because she's hungry — at least that's what she says. I think it's because she's nervous about what I'll say in my toast."

I raise an eyebrow. "Well, what do you expect? You pulled a practical joke on your twin sister in the middle of her wedding ceremony. I wouldn't trust you either."

Will laughs. "Point taken. But I promise to be nice."

I place my arm around his waist and walk with him toward the cake table. "Sorry, GQ. No one will breathe a sigh of relief until your speech is over."

"Come to think of it, I won't either. You go first."

"Me? I hate this kind of stuff," I protest as I hide my face in his chest.

"Okay, I'll get it over with, just so everyone can relax."

Will shifts to his public persona. It's almost as if his aura gets larger. His smile is a tad brighter, his laugh is louder, and he seems even more handsome.

He picks up a fork from the table and taps the edge of his class.

He holds the fork up to his mouth like a microphone. "Hello? Hello, is this thing on?"

The group of friends standing around the table

laugh. But Jude and Tasha see the commotion on stage and run down and hand my boyfriend a real microphone. I swear I hear Kendall groan in fear.

"That's better," Will says with a smile as he fiddles with the microphone. "Kendall, I want you to know I won't leave you in a lurch with this best man speech. I've been practicing for weeks."

Jameson salutes him with a champagne glass. "We know. That's what we're afraid of, bud."

Will winks at them. "I can't imagine why you all are so worried. It's not like I like to play jokes on my family or anything. Speaking of family, welcome to the family, Jameson. For those of you who don't know, Kendall is not just my sister, she's my twin. For years, I was her guy, her only guy. In high school, I used to make sure of it. I did my best to scare off anyone I thought was unworthy."

Kendall's jaw drops. "You did what?"

Will shrugs. "Someone had to look out for you. If anyone knew what teenage boys were like, it was me. Anyway, I digress. So, when you started waxing poetic about a new guy, my ears perked up."

Kendall rests against Jameson's muscular chest and sighs contentedly.

"For a while, I was concerned when she told me about this hot new computer technician in her life who she couldn't seem to connect with. If you'll pardon the pun, it seemed the two of you were always getting your wires crossed. Frankly, I didn't know how I would handle a situation where my sister had an unrequited love, especially with a guy the size of you."

Jameson smirks and chuckles.

"It's a good thing you guys worked out your differences, I was seriously thinking I might have to take a self-defense course to defend my sister's honor. But as time went by, I noticed a remarkable change in her. For the first time since I can't remember when, Kendie was smiling and practically effervescent. That's when I realized you weren't some run-of-the-mill more-brawn-than-brains kinda guy."

Jameson flexes his biceps and practically busts out of his tuxedo.

"Show off," Will mumbles, forgetting he's holding a mic.

"Anyway, every guy wants to see his sister with a man who helps her dreams come true and supports her to become a better version of herself than she ever thought possible. Thank you for being that guy for Kendall. Even though it's hard not being my sister's number one guy anymore, I'm glad she chose you as her heart's wish come true."

Will raises his glass. "Here's a toast to Kendall and Jameson: May your hearts always beat a little faster and your eyes light up when you see each other."

Kendall's eyes tear up as everyone responds, "Hear, hear."

"Aww, you're the best brother ever!"

Will grins. "Told you I wouldn't screw it up."

Jameson stands up and gives Will a huge bear hug. "You didn't. That was a class act. Glad to be part of the family."

Will comically adjusts his neck and back. "Thanks, bro. You saved me a trip to the chiropractor. Now, a few words from the other magnificent woman in my life, my girlfriend — and the maid of honor — Mariam Fischer. Isn't she gorgeous?"

I feel faint when the crowd applauds. Will frowns when he sees me sway. "Sorry, Mar. I forgot how nervous you were. You got this. I'm here if you need me."

Will literally stands behind me and puts his hands on my waist as he hands me the microphone.

My head pounds and my vision goes grey for a moment. I take a drink of my sparkling cider try to clear my head.

Clearing my throat, I forge ahead. "I'm not very good at this but I just wanted to thank you both for including me in your wedding. I'm shy and I tend to stick to my books and computers. It was fun to be part of such a great celebration. Kendall, I don't know very many people here, so I'm honored you treated me like a sister. I hope you and Jameson will remember this day as a celebration of your love story."

I pick up my glass. "I propose a toast to love stories which last forever."

Kendall stands up and runs over to me. I'm surprised at how agile she is in her bridal gown. She clinks her glass against mine. "Cheers to that!" Kendall places her arm around my shoulders and gives me a side hug. In a stage whisper, she says to the audience, "Besides, if I know my brother, it won't be very long until we are practically sisters in real life."

Brynley, the bridesmaid, gives me a thumbs up. "That would be totally awesome. It couldn't happen to a nicer couple."

I hung out with Brynley as part of the wedding

party, but I don't know her well. So, I smile and nod my thanks.

Will grins at her. "Pure class as always, Brynley. The guy who ends up with you is going to be so lucky."

Another wave of pain travels up my spine, through my neck and settles behind my left eye. My vision turns gray at the edges again. I turn the microphone off and hand it to Kendall.

"I need to go sit down," I whisper to Will.

Will weaves me through the crowd of people to some empty seats a few rows back. When I shiver with pain, he takes off his tuxedo jacket and places it over my shoulders.

The speakers screech with feedback as Norman taps the microphone. "I hope you don't mind if I say a few words."

Alarmed, I peer over at Will who is busy loosening his tie and rolling up his sleeves. "Will you be okay with this?"

Will nods. "I know what's coming. We talked about it over our male bonding session earlier. Surprisingly, I'm okay with it. It's their life and my mom seems ecstatic; just look at her."

Jameson claps Will's father on the back. "Feel free to take the mic, Norman. It's a day for love, Kendall and I don't have the only love story."

"I am so honored to be here today. I know I didn't earn the right to be here. It's only by the grace of God and the forgiving nature of my family I have the privilege to be amongst all of you. By all rights, my wife and my children should've told me to take a hike and never look back."

Jennie wipes away tears and then tenderly rubs Norman's back as he takes a moment to collect himself.

"But they didn't, so I got to see my baby girl marry a fine military veteran. I'm so proud of both my children. I didn't say that enough when they were growing up. I didn't say a lot of things back then. I didn't tell my wife, Jennie, how much I loved her. I didn't show it back then either. I did lots of terrible things I wish I'd never done. So, even though this saint of a woman is still technically my wife, I'd like to ask her to marry me again. I am a different man than I was when I left. I want her to get a chance to know the Norman Kordes I am today and decide if she still wants me. Jennie Winthrop Kordes, will you give us a chance to start over?"

"Of course I will. I've missed you so much," Jennie replies.

Norman makes a theatrical gesture of wiping the sweat from his forehead. "Not to push my luck or anything — but will you marry me again if you fall in love with the man I've become?"

Jennie stands on her tiptoes and kisses his cheek. "I make no promises, but your chances are pretty good considering I've never truly fallen out of love with you."

Justice Gardner walks over and hands Norman a card. "This group keeps me pretty busy officiating. Even though I'm retired, you might want to call ahead."

Norman shakes his hand. "I'll keep that in mind."

Will stands up and holds out his hand to help me up. Reluctantly, I stand but catch my heel on the leg of the chair. Will reaches out to steady me, but he doesn't know the whole right side of my body feels like it's on fire.

He grins at me with a mischievous light in his eyes. "It's been quite a day, hasn't it?"

My eyes widen with horror as I consider the possibilities.

Will pulls me toward where Kendall and Jameson are standing with his parents.

My head is pounding so hard I can barely see and I may throw up at any second. "Stop! Whatever you're planning to do, just stop."

Will turns back toward me. "What? You promised me a dance. It's time for the traditional first dance. Kendall wants the whole family on the dance floor. She's breaking with tradition."

"I'm sorry, Will. I love you, but I can't. I can't do any of it," I whisper as my legs give out and I collapse to the floor.

CHAPTER TWENTY-THREE

WILL

I PLACE A MUG of hot cinnamon tea in front of Mariam. "You want a muffin to go with that?" I ask as I hand her a handful of her medications.

She shrugs as she swallows her pills with a grimace. "I already had toast earlier. Not really hungry."

"You want me to run a bath or do you want to take a dip in the Jacuzzi?"

"William! You're driving me nuts. I don't have the flu. I have freakin' fibromyalgia. Stop hovering! No matter how hard you try, you won't ever make me better."

"I'm aware. I'm okay with that, but you don't seem to be. You want to talk about it?"

Mariam brings her knees to her chest and starts to braid the fringe on the edge of the blanket. "I warned you! I tried to keep you away, but you wouldn't listen. You kept coming around like an adorable puppy who needed a home. You were everything I thought you weren't. You were kind when I thought you would be cold. You were generous when I thought you would be self-centered. You were smart when I thought you would be shallow. You stuck it out when I thought you'd be long gone — when you should have been long gone. So, I did the dumbest thing I've ever done. I fell in love with you."

"Wait, I don't understand. Why is that dumb? I love you too. That's how it's *supposed* to work, right?"

"Yeah, for *normal* people. That's perfect! But I'm not normal or perfect ... and that's the problem."

"I don't remember asking you to be normal or perfect. Hell knows I'm not. I love you the way you are. Why is that so hard for you to believe?"

"Get a clue! I single-handedly ruined your sister's wedding. Actually, I'm two for two because I pretty much ran a sledgehammer through Phoenix and Zoe's too."

"Funny, I was there. That's not how I remember those events at all. My sister said she was grateful you were her maid of honor. You kept everything running smoothly and there was no drama. Both Jameson and Kendall were incredibly touched by the way you personalized the unity candle ceremony and made it unique. You even made my dad feel better about coming in at the last minute and asking to be part of the wedding. He didn't want to take over, but he still wanted to be part of it all. Your solution made everyone happy, including me. It was brilliant. But I know to expect those kinds of things from you."

"But my fibromyalgia flare ruined the first dance for you. You didn't get to be part of it because of me. I fell on the floor and made a spectacle of myself in front of everyone."

"You're not seeing this from my perspective. Most people were focused on Kendall and Jameson. The people who did see you fall, thought it was really romantic when I carried you to the house and took care of you. As far as the dance, I plan to spend a lifetime with you. We'll have plenty of chances to dance together. I'm not worried about it. I have two left feet, the newlyweds probably did better without me there."

"Very funny! I know you're trying to downplay all the drama my disease causes. But I have fibromyalgia twenty-four seven. It doesn't go away just because I have big events to go to or have other plans. I know the incident with Jennie was just one awkward conversation. But the fact remains: fibromyalgia is genetic. We have to talk about whether it's a good idea to have kids. We haven't even talked about that."

"Last I checked, lots of learning disabilities are genetic too, as is the propensity to have an addiction to drugs and alcohol. You've met my father — I've got risk factors in my family. Does that mean you shouldn't fall in love with me either?"

"No! I didn't say that. Those things aren't your fault," Mariam insists.

"So, if my genetic predispositions and health conditions aren't my fault, why are you blaming yourself for yours?"

"I'm not … really. Okay, so I am — which is stupid."

I raise an eyebrow and patiently wait.

"I just don't want you to regret your decision to love me when dealing with all the crazy effects of fibromyalgia gets old — trust me, it gets exhausting.”

“Mar, I know we’ve been together for almost a year, but it hasn’t been that long since you had to help dig me out from under a storage locker full of random crap. Remember how exhausting that was? Should I demand you not love me because my brain doesn’t operate like a typical person? Should I be frightened that one day you’re going to throw up your hands and decide the fight isn’t worth it? ‘Cause some days when you’ve figured out a contract in a second and a half and I’m still trying to read the first line, I wonder if I’m smart enough for you.”

“Of course you’re smart enough. You invent things. You run a charity which gives away hundreds of thousands of dollars. How could you say you’re not smart enough?”

“Exactly! You help me do all those things and you deal with all my craziness on top of it all. Not only that, you deal with pain I can only imagine. If you can love me with all my faults and weaknesses, why can’t I love you even though you have fibromyalgia?”

“I don’t know. I’ve had people promise they would love me before and they lied,” Mariam argues stubbornly.

“Yeah. They did, and they were jerks. The people who broke your heart and made you jaded were wrong.”

Mariam smiles a tearful smile. “They totally were.”

“I’m not those people. Aside from pulling a few office pranks and making you my unwitting accomplice in the wedding shenanigans, have I ever lied to you?”

Mariam’s expression grows wistful. “Well, there was that time you told me we had to go get your silver convertible repaired, and you actually took me to the beach for my birthday. I'll never forget that drive with the top down at sunset. It was one of the most romantic things I've ever experienced."

"So, aside from a small fib here and there, which usually works out in your favor, we've established I've never lied to you. I've told you over and over again that I love you and I want to spend the rest of my life with you. Why are we even having this conversation? Don't you believe me?"

"I do believe you. With my past, it's hard, but you're right. You never lie to me. I just don't think you understand fibromyalgia. The weddings were only the tip of the iceberg. Every time something big happens, good or bad, it makes me susceptible to a flare. It's a terrible Catch-22. The more I look forward to something, the harder it is for me to be there."

"So, we won't do a bunch of stressful events."

"But that's not fair to you. You love to be 'on'. You're bigger than life. You shouldn't have to live like a hermit because my body can't handle stress."

"Wow! I guess I've told you more lies than I thought. I don't like all that stuff. I'm good at it because I had to be. From a young age, I had to have great hustle because I had half a dozen side jobs to earn money to help my mom pay the bills. I was just a punk trying to pretend to be far older than I actually was. So, I was brash and acted like I owned the place. The truth is, I have to psych myself up for all that stuff. I hate it. I'd much rather be in my workshop creating things all by myself or in the kitchen with you learning how to cook."

"Seriously?"

"I swear. Part of the reason I founded the Heart Wish Foundation anonymously and kept Hallway Innovations low-key for so long is because I prefer to stay behind the scenes."

"Your cars and your flashy clothes seem at odds with that," Mariam remarks.

I chuckle. "Yeah, so sue me. Part of me still wants all the naysayers who thought I would be nothing but a troublemaking loser to know I've made something of myself. But that doesn't mean that most of the time I don't want to be chilling in my workshop wearing my sweats and a baseball cap."

"You're such a weirdo."

"I know, but I'm *your* weirdo. Will you marry me, Mariam Fischer? We can adopt a bunch of kids, or dogs, or cats — whatever suits your fancy. I draw the line at snakes though. I know it's not macho, but they creep me out."

Mariam chokes on her tea. "That's it? That's your big romantic proposal? No trip to Rome or the Caribbean or Paris? I take care of your books now. I know you can afford that."

"I could. But I know you, if I had made a big dramatic scene like that, that would've stressed you out. You would have worried about whether I should have wasted the money on the trip. So, here we are just sitting around having an honest conversation. I'm telling you that you are the most important person in my life and I will love you forever. I want to know if you are brave enough to go on this crazy journey called life with me? It's as simple as that."

Mariam's eyes tear up and she smiles at me. "Well, when you put it that way, it's the most romantic proposal I've ever heard. William Benjamin Kordes, despite my best intentions, I succumbed to the power of Will. I fell head over heels in love with you. If you're sure you can deal with the craziness I'll bring to your life, I am happy to become your wife."

EPILOGUE

MARIAM

"MELITTA! IF YOU WANT me to throw the ball, you have to let it go!" I instruct the rambunctious six-month-old Golden Retriever puppy bouncing at my feet. "Oh no, not in Dad's strawberry bed!" I gasp as she spits out her ball in Will's precious raised beds.

I grab the ball and toss it toward the grass, taking care to avoid the rose bushes and exotic mazes of flower beds.

Will has taken to gardening like nothing I've ever seen. Our yard looks like something out of a magazine. We have two greenhouses now. When I first met him, I would've never guessed he was such a homebody. He and Denny have been talking about grafting a few trees on the property to come up with some new varieties of fruit trees. At heart, my fiancé is forever an inventor.

Fiancé. That word still sounds odd to me, but under the bright sun, my ring sparkles like stained glass. I should've known Will wouldn't settle for just a casual engagement on a couch.

When my fibromyalgia flare was over and the weather got warmer on the coast, he hired Joe Summers to serenade us on the beach during a romantic dinner. He presented me with an engagement ring and told me that ordinary diamonds didn't suit me. Will gave me a ring with red rubies because he said that I boldly fight pain every day and still find love in the world around me. He says he never wants me to forget how beautiful I felt in the red dress Jordan created so, he gave me a little red to wear every day.

I adjust my baseball cap and lean back and squint at my latest watercolor painting when I hear the screen door slam. Melitta barks a happy little greeting when she sees Will.

Will looks around smugly. "It looks great out here, doesn't it?" He examines my painting. "Wow! That's a stunner. I can't decide whether I want to hang it in my office or give it to my mom for her birthday."

I shrug. "It's up to you. I can always paint another series. I think we should invite the family for the Fourth of July. You could cook some chicken on the barbecue."

Will looks at me with some concern. "Will that be too much for you?"

I shrug. "Not if you do the cooking. Besides, it's not like our family isn't over here all the time anyway. Your dad is doing a phenomenal job on your new Cobra."

"Yeah, I'm surprised he has any time to work on it with his new shop."

"I think Gwendolyn was afraid he might steal Denny away from the florist shop."

Will laughs out loud. "I don't know. The way I hear

it, he spends enough time at my dad's restoration shop he might as well work there."

Will's phone beeps. He looks down and checks the message. After several moments his eyes tear up. "You're not gonna believe this. We got government approval to begin trials with the university. We're going to be able to bring the laser technology to everyone — probably within the next five years. If this goes well, it could be a real treatment."

I stand up and hug Will. "Congratulations! I'm so proud of you!"

"You know what this means, don't you?"

"No, what does it mean?"

"If this works, it means I finally found a way to use my skills and my money to help you fight the pain of your fibromyalgia. An invention from Hallway Innovations may very well change the world! Not so bad for a guy who can't file his own taxes or read a software end-user agreement, huh?"

"Is it that important for you to a score a win on this one? I already know you are one of the smartest men I know."

Will nods. "You are the most important thing in my life. Pain makes you miserable. I can't fix that and it's frustrating. So, it's important for me to find some way to help. For me, this isn't about ego. It's another way for me to show you how much I love you."

I stand on my tiptoes, kiss him deeply and remind myself of the awesome power of Will.

Note from the Author

Dear Reader,

Thanks for reading my book. If you enjoyed reading about people who are not so stereotypical, then I've got good news…

… there's more.

Sometimes, your biggest challenge can be your biggest blessing.

Nothing in folk music star, Joe Summers's life is going according to plan. When he got engaged, he figured he would marry the love of his life and grow old with her.

Instead of wedding bells, life handed him a squirmy, crying baby boy. Life unfolded differently than he expected, but Joe became a teacher because he loves children. He would become the dad he never had. Brody would be his little buddy and love music as much as he does.

Brody is trapped in a world of silence.

His son never spontaneously interacts with anyone until he meets Brynley Meeker in the middle of the cereal aisle.

Joe is so busy trying to cope with the challenges of raising a child with a debilitating disability, he doesn't realize how lonely and isolated his life has become until a chance meeting changes everything.

Joe Summers touches the world with his words, is it possible Brody can change everything in Joe's world without saying anything at all?

~Mary

Because love matters, differences don't.

ACKNOWLEDGEMENTS

This book took a little longer than usual to write because my husband and I had our own real-life health challenges to deal with.

I'd like to thank my care provider, Antonia, for stepping up and doing more than her fair share during this difficult time.

Justin, you have been phenomenal and we are grateful for your better-than-average driving skills. Congratulations on your stellar grades this term.

Thank you, Dr. Brandon Crawford for giving me the proper medical diagnosis and treatments for my pretend patients. I am so proud of the work you do for your real patients.

Leonard, this has been a rough few months, but thank you so much for still supporting this whole writing thing. I couldn't do it without you.

When people find out about my background as a disability advocate, they'll often ask me which disability I think is the most difficult to cope with. In my opinion, an invisible disability like fibromyalgia is often more difficult to deal with than something like my cerebral palsy. People expect me to need help every once in a while. However, individuals who have an invisible disability such as fibromyalgia are often overlooked even though they may be in as much pain as I am.

I wrote this book to increase awareness of the daily struggles faced by individuals with chronic pain. I hope this helps people have open and honest conversations with the people they love. I appreciate everyone with fibromyalgia or chronic pain who bravely shared their struggles with me and gave me permission to use their stories as inspiration for this book.

I would like to thank my editor, Lisa Lee, for all of her hard work on this book. At times, it was disjointed at best. She did a great job of pulling it all together making it make sense.

Kathy, without your technical advice, this book would not be nearly as raw and honest. I can't thank you enough for keeping my work truthful.

Thank you to Kathern Watts who is my beta reader and research assistant extraordinaire.

Kudos to LJ Redding who finds new and creative ways to keep me on task and relevant to readers everywhere. Thank you for being a big part of the reason anybody knows who the heck I am.

Thank you to Kathy, Becca and Christina for being the typo and the grammar police. You strengthen my work.

Without fans, none of this would be possible. Thank you so much for supporting stories that are a little out of the norm. Because love matters, differences don't.

ABOUT THE AUTHOR

I have been lucky enough to live my own version of a romance novel. I married the guy who kissed me at summer camp. He told me on the night we met that he was going to marry me and be the father of my children.

Eventually, I stopped giggling when he said it, and we've been married for over thirty years. We have two children. The oldest is a Doctor of Osteopathy. He is across the United States completing his residency, but when he's done, he is going to come back to Oregon and practice Family Medicine. Our youngest son is now tackling high school, where he is an honor student. He is interested in becoming an EMT.

I write full time now. I have published more than thirty books and have several more underway. I volunteer my time to a variety of causes. I have worked as a Civil Rights Attorney and diversity advocate. I spent several years working for various social service agencies before becoming an attorney.

In my spare time, I love to cook, decorate cakes and, of course, I obsessively, compulsively read.

I would be honored if you would take a few moments out of your busy day to check out my website,

MaryCrawfordAuthor.com. While you're there, you can sign up for my newsletter and get a free book. I will be announcing my upcoming books and giving sneak peeks as well as sponsoring giveaways and giving you information about other interesting events.

If you have questions or comments, please E-mail me at Mary@MaryCrawfordAuthor.com or find me on the following social networks:

Facebook: www.facebook.com/authormarycrawford

Website: MaryCrawfordAuthor.com

Twitter: www.twitter.com/MaryCrawfordAut